To My

Kevin

Happy Holidays :)

Ava

Echoes from the Other Land

ECHOES

FROM THE

OTHER LAND

stories

AVA HOMA

We acknowledge the support of the Canada Council for the Arts for our publishing
program. We also acknowledge support from the Government of Ontario through
the Ontario Arts Council.

 Canada Council **Conseil des Arts**
for the Arts du Canada

 **ONTARIO ARTS COUNCIL**
CONSEIL DES ARTS DE L'ONTARIO

Cover design by Ingrid Paulson
Cover photo by Jonathan Schöps

Library and Archives Canada Cataloguing in Publication

Homa, Ava

Echoes from the other land : stories / Ava Homa.

ISBN 978-1-894770-64-4

I. Title.

PS8615.O486E35 2010   C813'.6   C2010-904993-4

Printed and bound in Canada by Coach House Printing

TSAR Publications
PO Box 6996, Station A
Toronto, Ontario M5W 1X7
Canada

www.tsarbooks.com

To Ehsan,
a wonderful, affectionate, supportive,
and appreciative friend and husband,

and
to all whom I love dearly.

CONTENTS

Fountain

ANIS LEANED AGAINST THE KITCHEN table. She squeezed and opened her left fist. The small pink pill had stained her palm. She put the tip of her right forefinger on the pill, swivelling it. Ali entered the living room, which adjoined the kitchen.

"Where've you put the bank passbook?" he called out.

Anis clenched her left hand.

"Where?" he asked again.

"I don't have it."

"Find it," Ali said and walked back to the bedroom.

Anis threw the pill in the trash basket and washed her hands. She walked out of the kitchen to the living room, picked up the head-scarf from the hook next to the outside door, and put it around her forehead, tying it tightly at the back. The headscarf was there for her to cover her head whenever she opened the door; this is how Ali made sure no man would see his wife's hair. Lately, Anis had been using the scarf to squeeze her head whenever it ached. She paused, went back to the kitchen, and picked up the watering can near the fridge. She went to the balcony from the kitchen and watered the flower pots.

Ali entered the living room wearing a suit. "Where are you?" he called. Scanning the room, he noticed a small object among the lilacs. Ali went to the coffee table and picked up the falcon-shaped plastic toy which had landed on the plant. "Falcons everywhere in this apartment!" he murmured. The balcony door opened and Anis emerged. "Headache again?" he asked. He threw the toy on the sofa and frowned.

She dropped the empty watering can down near the table and sat down at the computer in the living room.

Ali came closer and looked at the screen. Anis was writing a computer program in C++. He went to the kitchen, lifted the glass from the kitchen table, and drank the water. From the corner of his eye he watched Anis typing rapidly.

"Dirty dishes! Dirty dishes everywhere," he said, slamming down the glass in the sink.

Anis remained hunched at the monitor.

"Didn't I tell you to find it?"

She did not answer.

"I am talking to you," he yelled, going towards her.

"I said I didn't know," she replied.

"What do you know then? Huh?" He took the mouse and smacked it on the desk. "Who knows where anything is in this place?"

Her eyes were fixed on the keyboard, hand on her mouth. "You are the one who always has that bank pass thing, *Agha*," Anis said under her breath.

Ali hurried to the bedroom and took his Samsonite bag out of the closet. The booklet was inside. He went to the mirror and combed his hair. Examining himself, he raised a thick black eyebrow, inclined his body to the right and lifted his chin. He was patting his beard when he noticed a drawing above the mirror. It was a cat looking at a mirror, seeing a lion in its reflection. Ali removed it, tore it into pieces and put them in his coat pocket.

There was a knock outside. He perfumed himself, glanced again in the mirror, and walked out of the room. His friend Esi was at the door.

Anis had untied the scarf to have it cover her hair and was greeting the man. She had almost closed the door after them when Ali looked back. "Hey!" He put the pieces of the drawing in her palm and said, "Gimme your cell. Mine's dead."

Anis was staring down at her palm. "I'm expecting a phone call," she said, raising her head.

Ali pushed through the door, went to the small tea table next to the sofa, and picked up her cell. Anis stared at his dirty footprints on the floor.

After they had left the bank, Esi and Ali stopped in front of a juice shop. Ali ordered two glasses of cantaloupe juice and looked out at the street. Men and women formed two separate lines at the bus stop. An old man was buying bus tickets from the small booth next to the stop. His hair was white and there was a newspaper tucked under his left arm. A tall, young woman with a swarthy face, in a dark blue manteau and headscarf stood behind the old man. She bought a ticket and walked over to a tree across from the juice shop. She looked around, and then leaned against a tree, pushing back the sole of one foot and the back of her head against the trunk. Her book bag was clutched to her chest under her folded arms. She closed her eyes.

"Here you are." Esi gave Ali the glass of juice and followed his gaze towards the girl. "No eye candy."

Ali took the glass, continued looking at the girl.

"Want me to invite her here?" Esi asked.

"Nah." Ali took a sip.

"Let's have some fun."

"I don't feel like it."

"You sure?" Esi asked.

Ali nodded. "She's just . . ."

"Just what?"

"Nothing . . ." Ali took another sip.

"Doesn't she look like Anis?" Esi asked, looking back at the girl.

"Yeah . . ." Ali nodded. "And she looks . . . exhausted."

"Anis looked tired, too," Esi said, watching the girl carefully.

Ali was silent. Esi finished off the rest of his juice.

"Hey, don't choke." Ali laughed. He tried to chug his drink too, but a piece of ice got caught in his throat. He started coughing. Esi laughed loudly.

"What did you say?" Ali asked, his face red from the coughing.

"What?"

"What did you say about Anis?"

Esi put his glass on the counter. "I said she looked tired." He shrugged.

Ali gave the vendor a blue banknote and muttered, "She enjoys working her ass off."

They walked down Valiasr street. Traffic was at a standstill as usual. Noise and fumes filled the air.

"Hey, have you still got *Yalda Night*?" asked Alia, as they walked by the cinema, looking at the poster for *Cease Fire*. Two good-looking actors, a man and a woman, were leaning back against a tree trunk, frowning.

"*Yalda Night?*" Esi asked. "Sounds familiar."

"Where the woman goes abroad . . . then divorces."

"Oh, yeah. Didn't we watch it?"

"Yeah. Wanna watch it again?"

"I'll look for it," Esi said, observing Ali through the corners of his eyes.

They entered a park and walked down the stairs leading to a pond and fountain. They strolled around it. People had already filled the benches around the pond.

"How many times do you want to walk around this pond?" Esi asked.

"I want to sit somewhere and watch the fountain."

"The fountain? What's so interesting about the fountain?"

"I need to know what it has."

"What it has?" repeated Esi.

Ali nodded. "She loves it."

"Let me buy two sandwiches. What would you like?"

"No difference."

"Drink?"

"Beer."

"Islamic beer." Esi winked and left.

Two middle-aged women got up from a bench. One was on crutches and wore a loose milky manteau matching her hair. The other was fatter and helping her friend walk. Ali went and sat down on their bench and stared at the streams of water that rose, fell, and rose again.

A young couple stood near the fountain. The girl lowered her head and put both hands in her pockets. She appeared to be deep in thought. The boy put a hand on her shoulder and talked rapidly. Ali sighed, placed his elbow on the back of the bench, and stared at the couple.

Esi returned with a bag. He stood in front of Ali and looked down at him. "You look like death."

"Shut up."

Esi gave Ali his sandwich and drink and sat. "What's wrong?"

After a pause, Ali pointed to a grey shirt on a short man. "I bought a shirt just like that for my pigheaded boss."

"Mazaheri?"

"Yes."

"What did you do, finally, with him?"

"Nothing! I haven't been working lately."

"Really? I didn't know that."

"Yes . . . I've been spending savings so far."

"You're lucky Anis has a job."

Ali turned to Esi without warning and said sharply, "I use my own savings, man!"

"Really? What endless savings! Heh, have you been winning lotteries?"

"A few million dollars each time," Ali scoffed.

A young woman with a pink headscarf and a white manteau passed them, pushing a baby stroller with colourful animal dolls dangling from its top. Ali stared at her pink lipstick and matching scarf. She had bleached highlights in her black hair, strands of which showed from the front and back of her narrow headscarf.

"She'll be arrested for sure, as soon as she steps out of the park," Esi said.

"She deserves it, Esi. That's non-Islamic dress code!" affirmed Ali.

"Oh yeah, everyone has to be a Muslim in this country, even tourists," Esi said.

"When you are in a country you have to obey its rules."

"Screw a country where you're not free to choose even your look. Police now tell random boys in the streets to raise their hands: if the front of the shirt is not long enough to cover their stomachs, the boys get arrested. This country has no other issues except young people's hair and dress."

"Shhhhhh," Ali said. "Are you looking for trouble?"

The young couple passed them again. Ali slouched forward and gazed directly at them, one elbow resting on a leg, his chin in his hand.

"You remember the first time I showed you Anis?" Ali asked.

"Yes. I was behind that tree." Esi pointed to a big old tree near the fountain.

"How old can that tree be?" Ali asked.

Esi looked at Ali over his beer can and said after a pause, "You said she was your girlfriend."

"I was sure she would be. I knew something no boy knew. I knew her too well."

"What about her?"

"Well, she's a strange girl, the only girl from her island to have gone to university in Tehran."

"She played really hard." Esi crossed his legs.

"And she left her fiancé when she was in high school, a fiancé her father had pitched," Ali continued.

"How did you do it? Really." Esi turned to him.

"It's a secret."

"Come on. Not that you had any luck with other girls. And you don't want me to die a bachelor, do you?"

"Well." Ali shrugged. "You must look noble and kind—a true gentleman. She must think there is no one else like you." Ali winked. "She knew I was different from other men and I was the only one who knew how afraid she was of men and of marriage."

"So that's it. There is no one else like me." Esi smirked and drank his beer. "When her father issued his ultimatum . . ."

"Which one?" Ali jeered.

"The last one, you know . . ." Esi hesitated. "He'd never let her step on Qeshm Island again, if she married you . . . She's just incredible. I never thought she'd dare go against his will."

"He didn't hate me personally . . . just didn't want her to marry anyone not from the island—which is something she'd never accept," Ali explained.

Esi ate his sandwich and watched the fountain. The couple had approached the fountain again. A young boy in poor, dirty attire was now selling chewing gum there. Ali went back to his thoughts. Esi watched the shabby boy.

"The number of beggars increases hour by hour," Esi said. Ali was quiet. "Eat, man," Esi continued.

"I'm not hungry."

"Eat. Don't think about it."

"About what?"

"Whatever it is that you're obsessed with, lately."

"I'm not obsessed."

Esi drank his zero-percent alcohol beer. They were both quiet. Ali's gaze was fixed on the couple near the fountain. The girl had raised her face and opened her palms to catch the spraying water.

"Why are girls so in love with the fountain?"

"Not all of them are," mumbled Esi, looking at Ali who seemed agitated. "Ali!"

Ali turned to him.

"No woman can go abroad without her husband's permission. You know that," Esi said suddenly.

"What?" Ali turned to him. "What did you say?"

"You heard what I said."

There was a long silence.

Ali touched his beard. "How can you be that sure?"

"My friend, in the Islamic Republic of Iran a wife is like a personal tool, like a toothbrush." He laughed and drew nearer to Ali. "Seriously! Legally speaking, women have no right to step out of the house without their husband's permission, let alone go abroad."

"Absolutely! It's the fault of nice men like you and I that women can make themselves up and go out."

"I know. We're being too nice." Esi laughed.

"You think there would be no way to escape the law?" Ali asked.

"Canonically, commonly, and legally, no way."

Ali didn't say anything but kept looking at the couple and pulling at his beard.

"But . . . seriously! Let me tell you something. I'd let her go. I would, if I were you . . . trust me. I'd go myself. One is not always lucky like that, you know, to have a wife like that. You don't need to worry about English. You'll pick it up."

"Sure, I'll give her formal permission to go," Ali said sarcastically.

"PhD scholarship! Thirty thousand pounds! That's a lot of money, man. She's a genius!"

"How do you know all that?"

"I know, everyone knows. That's not something anyone would hide."

"I shouldn't have let her do a masters. My first mistake," Ali thought. "Uhmmm anyways, my father's ill. You know I can't go," he said.

"Say!" Esi exclaimed, swallowing a morsel. "Did I tell you I saw your father in Mellat Park yesterday? He had your athletic clothes on. He was running."

"Yes. He's a real sportsman."

"He's healthier than you, man." Esi took another bite and continued. "You were wrong to bring your parents to Tehran though. People are escaping this crowded, polluted, and expensive city nowadays."

"I'd love to leave this city. Anis refused to go."

"Seriously! Your father seemed much healthier than you."

Ali put both of his elbows on his knees and leaned forward. He touched his beard softly. "They can't come. Can they?"

"Where? England? You go and settle down first. You can invite them later. Not to worry."

"My dad doesn't want me to go."

"Has he said that?"

"No. But, I know it won't be easy for him."

"Come on! You've three other brothers who live in this city. They can take care of him."

"But . . ."

"What, man? What are you scared of? I can't understand why you don't get the hell out of this messed-up country," Esi said loudly. "A war might break out any moment. I'd leave here in a second with no hesitation, if I could. To anywhere, even Malaysia, even India. I mean it, man. I'd leave right now. At least you won't live with the fear of war, inflation, and the damn police every single minute."

Ali remained silent and stared straight ahead at some far spot. After a while he said, "You know, Esi, if something happened to my dad, I'd never, ever forgive myself, or that Anis. I can't abandon my father and my home like she did."

"Didn't she do it for you, though?"

"Shut up." Ali opened his bottle and downed his beer.

Anis was staring at the monitor. She had stopped at line twenty-four of her program. She rose from her chair, drew back the corner of the curtain, and looked out. A little girl in pink was hopping along the lane, talking to a man who was holding her small hands, smiling at her. Anis followed them as they slowly walked away until she could no longer see them. She opened the window, leaned out, and watched them until they disappeared again beyond the curve of the street.

She walked back into the living room towards the telephone, leaving the window open. The wind ruffled the white silk curtain. She put her fingers on the number pad, pausing after each number: 0 . . . 7 . . . 6 . . . 3 . . . She held the receiver to her breast while her dad's number went through. Then she hung up. She dialled the number again. Hung up. She stood up abruptly, hiding her face in her hands.

After a few minutes of pacing around the apartment, she put a CD with a picture of a sitar and violin on it, into the computer. She lay down on the carpet in the centre of the living room, hands open, staring at the ceiling. Anis breathed deeply and closed her eyes. For several minutes she remained motionless and listened to the music. A tear formed at the corner of one eye, which she wiped away with the back of her hand. Suddenly, she stood up and strode over to her bookshelf. She pulled down *Interpretation of Dreams* and searched for the word "dyspnea," finding nothing. Carefully placing the book back on its shelf, she walked to the computer, deleted some lines of code and started writing again. A few minutes passed and she stopped again. She clenched her hand against her forehead.

Anis got up and started pacing. She walked to the end of the kitchen and came back to the living room through the bedroom. It took fifteen steps. She paced rapidly, rubbing her left arm. She arrived at the phone, picked up the receiver and dialled three numbers. No answer. She dialled the same number again; then again. Finally someone at the other end said, "You have reached the Tehran Association for Mental Health Counseling Hotline. Please wait." Anis chewed on her nails. After several minutes, the same voice: "All of our counselors are busy at the moment. Please try again later."

When Ali opened the apartment door, Anis was about to leave.

"Look at that!" He frowned, closed the door firmly and stood in front of her.

Anis looked down at her black manteau and pulled her headscarf forward to hide the pile of hair on her forehead.

"You look like the peasant girls from your island." Ali slouched into the kitchen and drank from the water bottle in the fridge.

Anis bit her lip as if she were about to speak. Ali stepped back towards the door where Anis was polishing her shoes. His brow furrowed, the corner of his lip curled.

"What's wrong? Do I look pale?" Anis asked, turning her head towards the kitchen.

"Pale? You drown yourself in makeup."

"Makeup? I'm not wearing makeup."

"Your lotion, I mean."

"You mean my sunscreen lotion? I put it on in a hurry. It took me so long to finish the damn computer program."

"Where do you want to go?"

"You know where."

"Go wash your face."

"I'll sweat and it'll be absorbed anyway."

"I said, 'Go and wash.'"

"How can I wash off sunscreen?"

"Heh . . . you're scared your skin would get darker than this? Scared of losing your exemplary beauty, princess? Hah?"

Anis looked directly into his eyes. Ali began to play with his collar. Anis's eyes were level and hard. Ali sat down.

Anis went to the bathroom, opened the door and looked at her reflection. She rubbed her face, touched the dark spots under her eyes, held her face under running water and again rubbed her face. Her skin reddened. She smirked.

"What are you laughing at?" Ali was standing next to her.

"I didn't laugh." She gave him a serious look.

"I saw it. What're you smiling at?"

She didn't answer.

"What did you just think of and laugh at?"

Anis stepped out of the bathroom, her face dripping. Picking up the disk on the computer desk, she opened the front door. But Ali had followed her; he reached around her and shut the door, then came to stand in front of her.

"What do you suppose you are doing? Where are you going?" Ali asked.

"Nonsense! Nonsense!" She shook her head. "Didn't I ask you to come with me?"

"Why are you so happy?"

"You can come with me . . . right now . . . I can wait for you."

"I asked why you are so happy."

"Am I happy?" she shouted. "Am I? Are you blind or stupid?"

"What did you just say?" He pushed her. "What did you call me?!"

"Leave me alone. I'll submit this shit and will be back in an hour."

"Why don't you email it?"

"I told you, I'm supposed to pick up my check today."

"You're not going."

"I have to go."

"No you don't. They're not your husband. I tell you not to go. And you can't leave the home when I don't allow it." He shoved her backwards.

Anis put her hand on the wall, trying to keep her balance and swallow her anger. "I've promised to . . ."

"I don't want you to go out today."

Anis glared at him. "What do you think you are doing to . . . me?" Her chin quivered.

Ali stared into her black eyes. The eyes that he was trying to recall in the park were dewy now, eyes that were his life once and were, now. He smiled. Ali laughed and pulled her into his arms. "Oh, sweetheart! Just kidding, darling!" He held her firmly and caressed her head gently.

Anis peeled herself from his arms, opened the door, and left. Ali rushed to the balcony. He saw Anis open the door of the building and run. She ran as fast as she could. Ali stepped forward. His foot touched something and he felt it break. It was one of her flower pots and the falcon toy on it fell down from the balcony onto the street. When Ali raised his eyes again, he was not able to see Anis any more.

Wind Through My Hair

I LOOSEN THE TIE of my headscarf as I turn from Niayesh Highway into my street. My left hand on my throat, I unroll the window to let the air through my hair. The radio rambles on about the new law to make polygamy easier in order to protect the dignity of the family. Turning it off, I press play on the stereo and hum along with the song "Take me away."

Putting the car keys on the kitchen table, I toss aside the manteau and headscarf and shake my hair frantically. It strikes me then: "Why not call now?" Fishing the cell out of my manteau pocket, I look up the list of the most recent calls I've made: Liar; the Charlatan car purchaser; Reza's is third-last. My thumb on the green button, I do not press it.

I close my eyes, mouth, and nose with my fingers and submerge myself under the bath water. How to begin the conversation? On the way home from the hotel, pressing gear and brake alternately for two and a half hours, I have had more than enough time to clarify my thoughts. What seems easy in thought, becomes difficult in practice. But I should make the phone call tonight and then think about finding three million tomans to pay Liar so that he can help me get out of this Pigsty.

I push my head out of the water and cough, breathing quickly. Oh, God! I breathe deeply several times to relax. I'm exhausted, my eyes keep closing.

"Hilton Hotel is *honoured* to have you here, sir," I said this evening to that sharply dressed, good-looking blond, who looked about thirty-five. He was wandering around the lobby, carrying a medium-sized brown suitcase, and looking puzzled and tired.

"Oh," he smiled and came towards me. "I meant to go to the Evin Hotel. Taxi driver's mistake, I guess." A Russian/Polish accent, I assumed.

"No worries, sir!" I said, whirling a pen in my hand. "I guarantee a better quality of services here." Head tilted, I winked.

"I've booked a room there and—"

"Hmm . . ." Pen now in corner of mouth. "Let me see if we have a nice room to offer with a special discount for you!" He stared at my red lips. "Evin used to be a pretty good hotel actually." I leaned forward and he came closer. Unlike most men, he was not short for me. I whispered in his ear: "Not any more, I'm afraid."

He laughed.

"Lady, your man magnet always works," my manager whispered to me as I stared after the gentleman as he walked with the footman to the elevator.

"Take me away," I murmured.

16

"Pardon me?" the manager asked.

"I just said give me a break." I grinned.

Pushing my hands through the bubbles, I massage my tired "man magnet" calf muscles. Thirty years old in less than a couple of months. How much will that take away from me? I pour shampoo over my hair and rub it in. Maybe I should not be that picky about choosing a man?

Still in my bath towel, I lift up the jeans I had tossed off and fish out the cell, resolved to call Reza. Why do I always put my cell in my pockets? I dial Reza's number but hang up before it rings. I rub my eyes, take a deep breath and dial again. He's at Saman's. I say I will call later and return to the bathroom to dry my hair. When I turn off the hair dryer, I hear the cell ringing. I run back to the room and pick it up—no answer. There are three missed calls, all from Reza. I sit on the sofa and put my legs on the coffee table. Should I call now? What should I say?

A sudden vibration in my palm startles me.

"Reza, where are you?"

"Outside Saman's building. How are you?"

"I'm good, I'm good. Go back in because I might talk for a while."

"That's fine. I'm on my way home."

"Oh . . . okay. So, how's everything with you?"

"Things are okay, busy studying for the comprehensive exams with Saman. This man is a genius at math."

"You're hardcore, doctor!"

"Ha ha . . . Want me to come over?"

"Uhmmm . . ." I lift my legs off the table and lean forward, my forehead in my hand. Twisting my hair strands with my index finger, I notice that there's a rapid pulse at the back of my neck. I try breathing deeply, stand up, and walk to the window. Just get rid of the polluted air! I push aside the curtain and stick my cheek to the corner of the window pane and look at the city lights, the sky-scrapers, until my breath makes my vision of the outside blurry.

"Hello?"

"I . . . I'd rather talk on the phone, to be honest. It's already hard enough," I finally tell him.

"You don't need to worry. I'll be calm and cool in any case."

"I know, I know. And please be patient if I'm not articulate tonight."

"Sure. Hey, are you playing with your hair now?"

"What? Why?"

"I just pictured you doing so."

"Heh . . . No, I wasn't." I clean the track of my breath on the window with my forehead and glance down the street. A teenage boy is putting up a black flag on the wall of a building: the name Imam Hussein is printed on the flag in dark green. Dressed in black, he has a green headband with words written across it that are unreadable to me from this distance.

"Poor little boy!" I say.

"Me?" Reza asks.

"Of course not! Heh . . . I just don't expect this kind of thing in a nice neighbourhood, although you shouldn't expect otherwise in a country ruled by the 'Representative of God' on earth."

"What's wrong, Azar?"

"Nothing, why?"

"You must be mad at something, you're attacking the regime again."

"What?"

"What about the poor little boy?"

"That's so unfair, Reza. My political criticism is not an emotional projection."

"Haha . . . I was just kidding. So who's the poor little boy you were talking about?"

"Well, I just noticed that Ashoura month has started."

"So?"

"Nothing! I'm just reminded that we're still living in the Dark Ages."

"Oh, well. Wasn't Persia a civilization when the West was in its Dark Age?"

"So what? It's the other way around now. I'm afraid you were born a little late, Mr Patriot! This is not Persia any more, this is Islamic Pi— Republic of Iran and—"

"Deny our history and we're nothing."

"Well, live in history and think that Cyrus the Great is still running your country."

"Oh, isn't he? I heard that before, didn't believe it though."

"Not funny!" I say. "You're not supposed to make jokes in the month devoted to mourning your Imam's death." I look out the window again and see three men in the street, one of them elderly with white hair and beard, all dressed in black and busy setting up a tent for mourners. "I don't understand! Do these people really believe that crying and beating themselves up will purify their sins?"

"Aren't people free to believe what they want?"

"But they judge *me*. I don't really mean to judge them." I turn back from the window. "They scold 'evil' people who do not mourn a death—whoops—a martyrdom—that happened . . . when did this happen again? Two thousand five hundred years ago? I'm so sorry news takes so long to reach this country."

He doesn't answer. I breathe deeply and lean my head against the window. Oh my God, Reza must have been one of these young men, I realize. In that case, that annual masochistic carnival must have brainwashed him. And I? I never even wanted to look at narrow-minded people like that, let alone date them.

"Guess what I was thinking about tonight?" Reza asks.

"What?"

"Do you remember the first time we met?"

"Last year?"

"No, no, eight years ago, in the central library of the university."

"Oh, yeah!" I sit down on the sofa. "You were looking for the meaning of the title of some English book, right?"

"Ha ha . . . yes, and you asked me why I'd want to read the book if I didn't know what the title meant."

"I know. I used to be rude like that." I pull my hair in front of my face and look out the window through the spaces between the strands that reached my navel, like the bars of a cage.

"Ha ha . . . to be honest, I knew you long before that," Reza says. "The very first week you entered Tehran University."

"I remember the library, the way you were looking down while talking to me, like a good Muslim, heh!" I blow at my fake blonde hair, pushing away the strands from my face, though I can't see any more through them than before.

"I just wanted to be respectful."

"I find that pretty rude actually, although one should be used to stuff like that in an Islamic Pigsty."

He pauses. I lean my head back and flip the hair away from my face. Why do I never get used to the most everyday conventions of this country? But I am just as tired of our never-ending arguments as he must be.

"What harm has Islam done to you, Azar?" He asks.

I think I've offended him.

"Oh, nothing! Keep it out of the government and believe in whatever you wish. I just hate the air of superiority."

I am clawing at my head.

"One of our problems, I mean as Iranians, is that we blame the government for everything, even our personal problems."

"'Personal is political, political is personal.'"

"So, which book have you been reading lately?"

"Oh, shut up!" I can picture his face as he asks me this, scratching his beard and pushing one brow up, looking serious. "But seriously, when we met last year after all those years you were a completely different person. I noticed that because you were staring at me."

"Ha ha . . . I was pretty awkward. But I didn't expect to see you at all and you looked so—" A car honk drowns out his last word.

"So old, eh?" I should go to the beauty salon soon, before my white hairs grow too long and begin to show. "I didn't expect to see you either, actually. I never thought you would make friends with people like Saman and Sheida. You used to have your small religious community and that was it."

"Saman and Sheida are really nice—and unbiased."

"I'm not biased, Reza!" I keep my voice down to avoid starting a fight. "I've just had enough of the Islamic Dungeon and its brutal laws for women—"

"For everyone," he interrupts me.

"For me, being religious means accepting the regime and that's one thing I loathe intensely."

"But you figured out later that that's not true about many people, especially me, right?"

"Well, you do side with the regime at times."

"Me? Never Azar, never. Loving Iran and supporting the regime are two different things."

I pull my hair across my left shoulder and notice the dry and brittle strands. "Well, what I like about you is that . . . you know how Sheida can quickly come up with a reason to get angry even when nothing is really wrong? That used to make Saman and me stay quiet or end the party after an hour or so. Since you became a friend of ours, your sense of humour has lightened her up, all of us, actually."

"Thanks! We should've become friends seven years ago when I was younger and funnier."

"I wish," I whisper.

"Pardon me?"

"Nothing, nothing! Call me when you reach home."

I hang up and toss the cell onto the sofa.

Had I not ignored him eight years ago, things would be very different now. I sigh and go to the fridge. There is nothing there. I drink some water and kick the fridge closed, swearing loudly. I hunch up in my sofa. Who knows, though? Once the laws had offered him absolute authority over a wife, Reza might have become someone not too different from Jerk.

Who has been closer to me in the past year than Reza? No one, not even Sheida, let alone her fiancé. Reza is the first person I call any time I need help fixing my car or something in my apartment. But I don't let this intimacy create attachment. If I don't get together with him, Sheida, and Saman every now and then on weekends, loneliness would drive me crazy. But I'm sure I never act flirtatiously. If "they" didn't arrest people for committing the crime of hanging out with people of the opposite sex, or because our clothes, hair, or eyebrows don't look the way they want them to, we could go out instead of staying in. They are everywhere, even on the mountains. Over the last year, I have had a great time with my friends in Saman's apartment, playing games, watching movies, dancing, and talking for hours. The reason I always catch a ride with Reza is because he lives nearby, on the other side of the highway, and he is too religious to drink. We have to end our parties after two AM because not too many police are around then. Was I wrong to let him come over to my place after the parties? At least I made sure it was late enough for the neighbours not to see me, Allah forbid, letting a man into my home. But I have my most interesting conversations with Reza after parties, until five or six in the morning, when he leaves before the neighbours wake up.

I lie down on the sofa, hold my arm on my forehead, and stare at the only lamp hanging from the ceiling. Last Friday—oh I hate weekends and their loneliness—I hadn't seen Reza for two weeks and Sheida mentioned that he was depressed. Depression is very unusual for Reza, though a recurring event for me. He is the only one who can cheer me up when every now and then I lock myself in for a few days.

That damn Friday, I was standing by the oven, stirring soup, my mind wandering all over the world. I called on impulse and didn't even feel like justifying my call. His voice was very quiet and he was not at all surprised by my call. "What's wrong?" I asked. He wanted to tell me but couldn't, because he said it would drive me mad.

"Wait, does it have to do with me, then?" I asked.

"Maybe!"

"I promise. I won't be angry. Tell me . . . what's going on?"

"I can't say on the phone."

"Now or never." I hold a hand on my hip.

"At least let me think before I talk," he said.

"Call me back, soon." I hung up and tasted my soup.

I waited an hour. What was wrong with this Tehranian man? Had Jerk somehow found Reza and spoken to him, too, about me being the "aggressive, disobedient, and sexually cold wife who at the end broke his heart for another man"? How would Reza react to those lies if he ever heard them? Had my dad spoken to him about me being the bad girl he's ashamed of? Was I being fired from the hotel? Had anything happened to my mother? Had the government decided to ban people from leaving the country? Stupid, stupid thoughts! None of these would make him depressed. But, he said it had to do with me.

I forgot about eating and decided to go to a park and play badminton with Sheida to get rid of what was preoccupying me. Before I could leave, Reza turned up at my door. I let him in immediately, partly mad at him for risking coming over during the day, but I didn't say anything. I called Sheida and cancelled our plans.

I put some snacks on the coffee table for him. "Oh, I have ice-cream and biscuits as well. I went shopping this morning." I smiled.

"Would you please sit down for a moment?"

"I don't really feel like eating ice-cream. I want a hot drink, what about you? Hot chocolate? Cappuccino? Coffee? Tea? Green tea?"

"No, thanks."

"Then let me make myself a hot chocolate and I'll sit down. So, do you want to watch a movie?"

"Not really."

"I have an awesome movie: *Thou Shalt Not Commit Adultery*. It's brilliant, I love it." As I went to him, cup in hand, I heard footsteps at the door. "This next-door neighbour of mine is a busybody," I whispered. "I'm used to duping people like that though."

"For sure. That's your skill."

"Honestly, I pay two-thirds of my income to rent this cramped bachelor's where I expect people don't have their noses in each other's lives. But even here there's one of those fools who watches single people to make sure they don't sin and arouse Allah's anger." I crossed my legs and took a sip.

He was pushing his toes back and forth, rubbing the small red flower on the Persian rug I'd borrowed from Sheida.

"Anyway, I told the neighbours my parents are in Australia and that I'll soon join them. Heh . . . Australia, my ass! They've never been out of Asia and that was before the revolution. Nowadays, they can't afford to visit Tehran. I miss them badly."

He was silent, shaking his right leg.

"I should've never left Tehran after graduation," I added, and leaned back on the sofa. He was sitting at its other end.

"I thought you'd be back the year after. I heard you were thinking about doing your Master's."

He stretched his arm on the sofa towards me.

"I was. And at the same time, I was fed up with school and

loneliness, mostly. So I said I would take a year off, live in my hometown, you know, my parent's home, relax for a while, work part-time, make some money, you know, to be able to rent a place in Tehran and study for the graduate school entrance exam. I couldn't stand the dirty, disgusting dormitories any more, living with six stupid girls in one room, ahhhhhh, crazy!"

"How long did it take?" he asked.

I looked at him, surprised.

"I mean from the day you went back home to the day . . ."

"Oh, three months!"

He got up and walked to the window. "How could you make such an important decision in just three months?" he said, with his back to me.

I pushed my body to the edge of the sofa. "Things happen, Reza. The town's environment. I was done school and . . . the mentality of the town pushes you. How long can a single young woman keep saying no? How on earth can a female at that age, who is done school too, remain single? Being single has one and only one meaning: no one wants her—therefore there is something *wrong* with her. You don't understand! You're from Tehran. People in small towns drive you nuts . . ." I kept my voice low again to make sure the neighbours didn't hear me, leaned my head back on the sofa and closed my eyes. "Jerk promised that we would go abroad to continue our education together and he ended up not letting me go to work because there were 'too many men' in my department."

Reza walked back and sat down on the sofa next to me. I could feel his gaze upon my face but I didn't open my eyes. "Everyone pushed me then, but when I wanted to end it, no one supported me. I thought through that for more than two years."

"For more than two years?" he said loudly, and I was concerned the neighbours would hear him. "That means you were happy with him for less than a year? Only?" He bent towards me.

I opened my eyes and stared at the steam rising from my cup, disappearing but still offering me the odour of hot chocolate. It was six months after the golden days when Jerk grabbed my cup and poured its contents into the sink, banning me from hot chocolates so I could "get into shape."

"No one supported me, not one person from all those who had pushed me into the tempting trap," I said.

"Sheida is supportive."

"She is, but she has no influence over my parents. A second-cousin, living far away . . . and her situation is so different; she lives in Tehran."

He was shaking his head. I couldn't stand anyone blaming me for those damn three years of torture. I turned off the lights. "Hey, let's watch a comedy to cheer us up."

I played the only DVD I had, a Mehran Modiri movie that I hated. Reza was not paying attention to the movie either. I faked a laugh every now and then, which seemed to distract him from his thoughts. His presence was unusually heavy and bitter. I stole another glance at him. Reza was small and extremely skinny, with a big nose, unshaven face, large ears, and a huge birthmark under his chin. How did all these seem lovely to me at one point? Jerk was tall and well-built and I hated him with a passion. My eyes checked the clock frequently. The lovers got married and that was the end of the movie.

"It's over," Reza said.

"No it's not over; it's the beginning of living happily ever after." I stood up.

"Please don't turn on the lights. I need to talk to you."

The sun had already set. I sat down and examined my painted toes showing through the slippers. I could feel his gaze upon my face again, and dared not look back. He was silent and so was I.

"I don't really know if I should say this. If I talk, I might damage our friendship but if I don't, I might lose you for good," Reza said.

"You're the one person I've been able to talk to, better than anyone else."

"What are you talking about? Do you want to go to Sheida's place?"

"I don't feel like it at all."

"Let me make some tea," I said, standing up.

"Listen, please."

I sat down again.

"I don't know where to start or how to put it."

"You don't have to talk."

"I want to."

I remained silent.

"Please don't think I'm going to take advantage of our friendship or your trust in me," he added after a long pause. "I had feelings for you from the very beginning; even before we became friends. I wanted to mention them but you were friendly and I was enjoying your company and getting to know you, and waiting for a chance to—"

"What made you change your mind?"

"Azar, I'm not stupid. I notice when men hit on you and I see how you neglect them so I was not really worried till two weeks ago when the hotel manager asked for your hand."

"But I rejected him."

"I know, but the thing is that it made me think 'what if she had said yes? What if she says yes to someone?' That would be too big of a change in my life. Do you understand? I thought if we don't get closer, we might get too far away."

"And if a relationship starts . . . what would it . . . lead to?" I asked, twirling strands of hair around my index finger.

"What is usually the result of a relationship?"

"But we're so different, Reza. I mean we get along pretty well but our backgrounds are extremely different."

"Well, as long as we get along!"

I had thousands of reasons to say no and he still managed to convinced me. He said he was not a controlling man, he did not mind my beliefs or lack of beliefs, if I didn't mind his. He promised to take care of me and said I could end the relationship anytime I wanted to.

"Oh, Reza, what in this messed-up country attracts you?" I said when he was about to leave at three in the morning. "I know, I know . . . your roots. What is a root, for God's sake, why don't I have any?"

"You're just taking them for granted." He closed the door again.

"Our roots are in the wrong place, then. We'll root again in a better place. Australia is a wonderful country and has lots of immigrants. We won't be too out of place there. And how many of our educated friends are still here? Everyone has gone to Canada, Europe, America."

"That's exactly what they want, Azar, if people like you and I who don't comply and can think for ourselves leave, then they can rule the rest easily." I could feel his breath on my face.

"There is no use staying here. Struggling to survive, we'll become as corrupt as the regime and it will be so gradual that we won't even notice. Look at me! Was I like this before? I am a liar, a manipulator now. I live like a refugee in this neighbourhood, this city. I don't even know what I'm escaping from any more."

"If you're a refugee here, sweetheart, what will you be in Australia? *If* you can actually make it," he said staring in my eyes and pushing my sweaty hair away from my forehead.

"A refugee again! . . . but I'll breathe, I'll feel the wind through my hair, you don't understand." Yet I craved to put myself in his arms.

"Your frustration is mainly due to your current situation, which will change. This is your home, Azar. After all, you're someone here," he said, robotlike.

"Oh, I am so so irrelevant in this country. I have no home . . . I am homeless like the wind." I felt like I was about to faint.

"We'll be fine together, we'll resist together," he said.

I was shivering, all of a sudden it was cold.

"Calm down, my darling, calm down," his hands on my cheeks.

"Don't treat me like I'm a pathetic hysteric." I pushed his hands away. "You're not a patriot or an intellectual or anything like that. You're just a coward and all you care about is yourself." I shut the door on him, hands on my throat, stifling a cry.

The vibration in my lap startles me once again.

"I'm home now," Reza says.

"All right." I get up, stumble to the fridge with a dizzy head and take out a bottle of beer. "Liar has asked for three million tomans more," I say out of nowhere.

"Your lawyer? Didn't you give him a million a month ago?"

I turn off the light, walk to the window and look out at the sky-scrapers.

"Hello?"

"Listen, Reza!" I turn my back to the window, peeling off the skin on my lips.

"Are you okay?"

"Oh, I'm a bit . . . just . . . I didn't really sleep last night and I'm sorry for yelling at you the other day."

"That's all good, I understand, it was my fault, a terrible time to lecture."

"Reza . . . I really appreciate your understanding."

"Why didn't you sleep?"

"I don't know, actually. I heard . . . or I dreamed that I heard someone walking about the apartment. I woke up and after that the sound of my own heartbeat wouldn't let me fall asleep."

"I wish I could do something for you, Azar. I mean, I can, if you just let me."

"Listen, Reza! You're a wonderful man. You have qualities I've always admired and longed to have. Like, you have a strong per-sonality, and morality . . . and you have this unique ability I love, you're able to laugh at almost everything, all the hardships." I pause for a second, waiting for his reaction. All I can hear is his quick breathing. "And I . . . you know . . . am alone in this big, brutal city . . . in the whole world. I have no one. I would love to have a man take care of me."

He laughs. I can't tell if it's out of happiness or nervousness. I lean to touch the flowers by the window. Hasn't a year of friendship been enough for you to see that he's a man you can trust and rely on? I ask myself. After all those ups and downs, here I am turning my back at the window that opens to a city where twelve million people live, wondering if I can survive here. After all, I'm somebody that other women fear because they think I'll seduce their men; but men want to take advantage of me, and when they are rejected, they humiliate me and gossip.

"Azar!"

"Mmm . . . My father's sick and Mom wants me to visit him." I claw at my hair. I'd better say it now.

"You should certainly do that."

What does Reza know? He never understands me. He's a man, he's from Tehran and he has a protective family. My father doesn't want to see me. He'd rather see me die than make him *bi aberoo*, ashamed. Jerk was a good husband: "wealthy and charming," so they say, and not that bad after all for laying a hand on me every now and then and fooling around. That's pretty normal for a man. *Why then do normal things lead me over the edge?*

If I could trust Charlatan to sell my car, I could give Liar his money. I open the window and shake out my hair. The polluted breeze makes me want to vomit. Reza is breathing heavily on the phone.

"Yeah, like I said, it was a very difficult decision to make and I thought deeply about it." I close the window, try to swallow an annoying lump in my throat that deepens my voice.

"Don't worry. I can handle it. I can control my feelings no matter how strong they are. Just give me good reasons."

"Good reason? I devoted three years of my life to Jerk, who was a dream man and was crazy about me, and who ended up . . . a vampire." I choke on my beer.

"I can wait! We'll be the same old friends and won't mention anything, till you think you're ready."

"Ahh, no. I mean, if you wait, that would mean an unstated commitment . . . And one thing that creates a huge gap between us is not our philosophies of life, it's the fact that you've never even dated a girl, while I—"

"That's the thing!"

"Well, the way I see this difference . . . it's like . . . how should I say this . . ?" I sit down on the floor. "Imagine two people trying to build a house. One is young, energetic and optimistic whereas the other has already built a house that's been destroyed—and she's under the rubble! The effort these two people put into the new construction isn't the same. I mean, I know myself, I'm bitter, wounded, shattered, I overreact . . . I wouldn't date myself."

He becomes quiet and this drives me crazy, I dare not even call his name. What am I doing to him? To myself?

I barely hear him. "Just leave me alone for a few days. When we meet again, please act as cool as usual, as if nothing has happened at all, and please don't let anyone know what's been going on."

"All right, sure," I whisper.

"I agree with the second reason," he adds. "I don't really care what else happens in my life. I'm indifferent to everything now, even the biggest catastrophe—"

"This is not a catastrophe, though; it is avoiding a catastrophe!"

"For you, it's nothing. A silly man wanted to enter your life and you pushed him away. You treated me nicely and rationally and I am grateful for that."

"That's not true, like I said, I like many aspects of your character and it was not easy to decide."

"You say that just to be nice. I'm an insignificant person who grew strong feelings for you that you didn't value. Nothing changed in your life. I'll deal with this easily though, easier than you think."

I open my mouth to say something. Instead, I punch and punch my forehead.

"But this failure had one good point for me."

"This is not a failure, Reza." I beat the bottle on my knee rhythmically.

"Whatever! When me, my friends and family were talking . . . years ago . . . every man said they'd never want a girl who has dated even once, but I was like, 'No, I don't care about the past,' and I proved to myself that I had not lied."

"Excuse me?"

He didn't answer.

"What did you just say?"

"I've been thinking about this for years. I'd never say this . . . but my older brother's wife was a similar case, and since then, about ten years ago, I've always been asking myself if I'd be able to do the same thing. I've realized now that I could."

"Hold on a minute, for God's sake! What are you talking about?"

"See! In any case, you are . . . I'm a man who has never touched a girl before and you are—"

"You think you're a saint, a superman, and me a criminal?"

"No, I'm sorry. I didn't mean it like that . . . It's not my thinking, it's society's."

"Society's? Not yours?"

"I mean, I never thought I—"

I press the red button. Grabbing my manteau and headscarf, I run down the stairs and jump into my car. I should call Liar right now; no, call Charlatan first. I must make a phone call, dial Liar's number and leave him a message to pick up his cheque tomorrow morning from the hotel front desk. No, I will ask Sheida to call him, I will ask her to call Charlatan as well. I must call now, I must. I press down on the gas. The lights of a police car flicker in my rearview mirror. I tuck in the loose strands of hair under my headscarf and tighten its tie.

A River of Milk and Honey

EVENING.

"Every relative is willing to donate as much as they can." I recognize Ronak's voice, my aunt.

"I know, but it's a high-risk surgery. What can I say? How can I make a decision like that for her?" That voice is Mom speaking.

"Trust God, dear."

"What've I done to deserve this?" Mom asks. "For which sin?"

Same old questions. I lean my head against the hallway wall. Which sin? Whose sin? Who pays for whose sin? Sometimes I wonder if God hates all the people in this city, all the people who live on the border of Iran and Iraq. My father says Sanandaj is a city of revolution and mass murder, tyranny and genocide. I was in my mother's womb when the war broke out and eight when it was finally over. I do not know what sin these people committed to deserve such horror but I know that God does not ever answer my prayers. Maybe He will in the afterworld.

"God is testing your faith," Ronak says.

Pushing the door open quietly, I tilt my head so as to peek into the living room. The two women are sitting on the handmade carpet, leaning against the new Kurdish cushions. Ronak takes a sip of her tea and notices me in the crack of the door. "Sharmin is a sweetheart," she says, raising her voice.

Mom's white headscarf that she wears during prayer has slid onto her shoulders and her salt-and-pepper hair is messy. "Her situation wouldn't run me down, if she was, at least, a boy," Mom says. Placing a hand on her hip, she winces.

"Sharmin, dear, come here," Ronak says. "You look nice in that shirt, darling."

Mom coughs and pulls the scarf over her head. I hobble over and sit next to Ronak and hide my head behind her shoulders, twisting my fingers into the hem of my blue shirt.

From her purse, Ronak takes out a book with a red cover. "Because you finished reading the last book," she turns her head to me, smiling. "You deserve a new one."

Good Stories for Good Kids 2. On the cover is a sketch of a young girl in a headscarf, across from a boy. I grab the book and limp hurriedly towards my room.

"Do you want to eat now? Your dad won't be in tonight," Mom calls after me.

"Not hungry," I say over my shoulder, and close the door and throw myself onto the bed. I open the book and position its corners on my ears.

Weekend. My uncle's family will visit us and I pray that Azad will be with them. Mom says he is a man now and does not go out with his parents. When I am on the rooftop waiting for the days to end, I often see Azad in the neighbourhood with his friends. I do not call out and he does not look up. I have a feeling that Azad will come over today, if it's God's will. Please, God!

Afternoon. The shampoo slowly slips to the corner of my mouth. The bitter taste. I close my eyes. It's not hard to imagine myself emerging from the River of Milk and Honey, luminous wings open. Azad passes by and stares. Gathering my wings behind me, I walk elegantly in a white dress towards a garden of red roses, pretending not to see him. A breeze blows through my hair. When I get to the garden, I turn and beckon to him; he has a look of adoration in his eyes. He runs to me. We walk together through the garden, hand in hand.

I begin shivering. The water always gets cold fast—to wake me from dreams, I think. No, "to save gas," says Dad.

My underdress and puffy pants are silver. I pull on the Kurdish dress, bright red and plain, with embroidery, which Ronak gave me last year. She bought it for me in Iraq—the only dress I have that Mom hasn't tailored. I choose to wear my short-sleeved silver vest, which I have decorated with white sequins and glass beads, tying the long tails of the sleeves behind my neck. The loose fit hides my noticeable breasts. I loop a belt around my waist and rummage through the dresser for a red headscarf and come across a vest of Mom's that's ornamented with sparkly charms, traditional amber, red and black beads, and gold jewelry received as dowry. In the last drawer, I find her belt, made entirely of gold lira coins connected and dangling. I have never seen my mother wear the vest or the belt. Mom and my aunts always wear dark-coloured, plain Kurdish dresses with long-sleeved vests and little or no accessories. I, too, do not like to make God angry by showing off. And though I hate covering my thick and wavy hair, nobody should pay for my sins.

I am trying on the headscarf when Mom appears between me and the mirror. She frowns at the messy knot I have made of the scarf and lifts a black scarf from the drawer: "This black one will make your face look smaller."

I examine her frowning face and then my own face in the mirror. It's nothing like a monster's. I am loveable.

"Take it," she sighs.

"I hate black." I move towards the door.

She drapes her arm around my neck and whispers in my ear: "Darling, everything will be fine after the surgery. I mean if your irresponsible father ever cares for his family."

Driving his truck between Iran and Iraq, Dad is never home but he is not irresponsible. He is kind and never talks about surgery. She pats my head. Turning my head, I search her eyes for something I cannot find. I push her hand away, and shuffle away as fast as I can up the flight of stairs to the rooftop.

I sit in my corner, in my chair. There is a blanket folded over the back, which I wrap around my body and over my head. Here, under the blanket, I see again men with thick glasses and green attires cutting my chin, like in the nightmares I have that I have never talked to Mom about. Azad is the only one to whom I will tell these things.

Footsteps. I feel a presence and steal a look from under the blanket. Azad is standing there and it is not a dream. Hands in his back pockets. I drop the blanket. Azad sees my uncovered hair. I am trembling. He has lost weight; the skin under his almond-shaped eyes seems darker.

"Sharmin!" He says my name in his deep, strong voice. "I knew you would be here! How're you?"

I blush and clumsily smile; my entire body pulses.

"May I?" He rocks my chair, chewing on gum, his eyes fixed on the Awyar mountains in the distance. "Exams, exams! I'm not in the mood to study whatsoever."

I would be finishing high school in two years if I were still in school.

"You're lucky, Sharmin! Rocking, watching pretty neighbours all day." He chuckles.

Azad talks rapidly, like always. Mom says he has changed, but for me he is very much Azad. He has the habit of pulling his left ear when excited. I've wanted to tell him how much I hated the school, the kids, and the teachers. I've wanted to tell him that I know why they hated me at school—because their heads were small and because they said I could not learn as fast as the others. But I've wanted to tell him that I am not stupid. I've wanted to tell him all my secrets.

"I'm going to enlist in the air force next year, in Tehran."

"Air force?"

"I'll make a good pilot, don't you think?" He winks.

"You'll fly people around the world?" I ask. I want to ask him if he remembers our childhood games, during the war, when he would take me around the world in his plane.

"Ha ha, no, war pilot. I know you have a gorgeous neighbour," he says before I get to say anything else, and he smiles mischievously. "Do you know which is her bedroom? Do you think she sleeps by herself?" He turns his gaze away from the neighbour's house and looks into my shocked expression. "Shaho, our other cousin, is in love with her, too. Her beauty is fascinating," he adds, to explain himself. I tell myself how glad I am that he still feels close enough to me to share his secrets. He knows that I will keep them to myself. But my throat has constricted. No one else is Vengeance like I am. "Her name is Kazhal," he says, and walks towards the edge of the roof, bending over it to peer across at the house on our right. "Rhythmical step, appealing makeup, large breasts, flat belly, big lips, God, she's incredible, just incredible," he says as if reciting a poem.

I've wanted to show him that no one has my hair.

Evening. Azad has left. "No one else is Vengeance," I say out loud, rocking back and forth in my chair. I look at the house on the right where a family has recently moved in. Unlike ours, it was built after the war so it does not bear the scars. This is the way the city looks: modern, chic buildings next to the old ones with their plastered-over bullet holes, next to others left to rot.

A child's voice in the alley calls for her mom. I hobble to the edge of the roof. It is my little neighbour on the left, Shilan. She is wearing a beautiful pink-and-white dress going down to the knees, with a frilly skirt and sleeves, like the ones in the pictures on the wall of my room. In one little hand, Shilan holds a bag containing three eggs. Her mom appears at the window and tells her to be careful, eggs are fragile. She looks up, sees me, and smiles. I wave at her. The eggs fall from her hands.

"Ah!" her mother cries and follows Shilan's gaze to my face. I quickly move away from the roof edge. "Oh, dear! Come in, sweetie," she says soothingly to her child.

I swallow the lump inside my throat. I should have known that Shilan's mother would see my oversized face anyway. Limping back to my chair, I press my chin with a palm; it is too big, way too big. Why doesn't Mom call me downstairs? Is she cooking or cleaning? It has gotten darker and colder, and fewer people walk about. My fingernails have turned white. I crouch down, kick the blanket and cover my scary face under my arms: God's Vengeance.

Kazhal is blessed. Azad had forgotten to mention that she has long black hair like mine that shows from the back of her black school headscarf. I imagine her legs are like those of women on magazine covers before the revolution, which I once found stacked in the basement and Mom got mad at Dad for keeping them. "What if *Komiteh* show up at the door without notice and find the pictures of these accursed women? Are you looking for trouble?" she asked him and burnt them all. But I still remember those women. Mom said, besides, no one is that perfect and those are only pictures. But Kazhal is real, although all you can see is her face and hands in her public outfit—but you can tell by the number of men who want her that she must be perfect. She has swum in the River of Milk and Honey; her mom is a chaste woman. Kazhal is not Vengeance.

Watch her at noon when she comes home from high school, anxious and tired. Boys follow her to the alley every day, this time five, two walking in pairs, one by himself. I recognize three of them. The second pair isn't from this neighbourhood. The two boys in front walk faster to get closer to her. One is tall, has a bit of moustache and looks excited. He suddenly picks up his pace, passes her, and clumsily drops a small piece of paper on the ground by her feet. Probably his phone number. She looks around to make sure none of the neighbours see her and then bends and picks it up.

I never see her not surrounded by high school boys. That's why she is infamous, Mom says. None of the boys are as attractive as Azad. Kazhal does not talk to any men in public, and the young men remain a few steps behind her when a *Komiteh* turns into the alley. Mom says that the police arrest couples who talk in public unless they can prove they are immediate family. People say that they hate *Komiteh* because they are constantly harassing everyone, but I see that people fear each other more than they fear the police.

Kazhal quickly tucks her loose strands of hair under the headscarf. She is a few houses away from her place when a *Komiteh* stops in front of the young men and an officer arrests the one walking alone, for his long hair, I suppose. My dad hates men with long hair, too. I don't.

Kazhal runs to her door and holds her finger on the buzzer. I crawl to my corner and look at myself in the broken mirror I found in the waste basket in my mother's bedroom. Dad says people go crazy if they look in the mirror too much. He hates it if I dress nice or talk to any boy, even Azad. "Are you making yourself up so that men can give you dirty looks?" he yelled at me once when Ronak did my hair. I rock and stare at my huge lips, play with the hair over my shoulder and think that it is really good that Dad is away most of the time.

"How's my girl?"

"Hello." I hide the mirror. I am scared although I recognize Ronak's voice.

"How do you like the new book?" she asks.

I am too embarrassed to tell her that I have not even looked at it. I twist the fingers of my hand in my hair and bite my lip.

"Want me to comb it for you? I've brought a brush."

I smile. She comes to stand beside me and combs my hair.

"They just arrested a boy," I say. "He was chasing the girl next door. She is beautiful. All the boys want her."

Ronak pauses, grabs my chin in her hand and turns my head up towards her. "Beauty is a misery, sweetie," she says looking into my eyes.

There are wrinkles around her eyes. Younger than my mom by six years, everyone thinks she is older. When young, Ronak was so beautiful that she was given away at sixteen. Her husband was hanged after the war so she was able to continue her education and now she teaches at a high school and lives a block away. I imagine her without wrinkles. Beautiful.

"Kazhal usually goes out with her mom in the afternoon," I say, turning back to look in the direction of Kazhal's house. I wonder if she got home safe. What has happened to the boys and to the one who was arrested?

"Just stay with me this afternoon," I say.

Ronak has too much to do but she stays anyway. We sit on the wall of the rooftop and peer over. Soon we see them leaving the house. Kazhal's mother is shorter than Kazhal and wears a black manteau and scarf as well as a frown. When they pass our house, Kazhal does not glance up at the rooftop. There is no one else in the alley except Shilan's father, stepping out of his car, a Renault 21. He ogles at Kazhal. Her mother pulls Kazhal's headscarf forward to cover more hair. She pulls away from her mother, who shakes her head.

"Heh . . . the mother thinks the poor girl will not attract men's attention if her hair was covered," Ronak smirks.

"But her manteau is too short, barely reaches her knees."

"No matter what she wears, men will stare, and women will blame her. They must prove together, but each in their own way, and in spite of the other, that no beauty is chaste."

"Between all these boys who are after her, one must have won her heart, at least. No one knows which one, though," I tell her.

"That's not what I mean," Ronak sighs and walks back to the roof door.

Azad told me he had heard from lots of boys that they had been with Kazhal. He found out later they were bluffing. One of the few sentences I spoke that evening was to ask if he ever found out whose girl Kazhal had been. He said he hoped no one's. "I don't want a second-hand girl," he said. "No one wants a second-hand girl!"

"Oh, she, Beauty, is the poor thing neighbours talk about everywhere, in buses, taxi stations, grocery stores, everywhere," Ronak says, standing at the door. "Some say that she must've gotten plastic surgery. The lady next door believes she must be using special American make-up to give that sparkle to her cheeks and forehead."

I take one last look across at the alley. Azad is recognizable from afar. He walks in front of Kazhal's house every evening, and there he is. He does not see me.

✄

Birds can find lots of food these days but I still enjoy crumbling dried bread for them. They are not scared of me. I am standing near the edge of the roof with crumbs of dried bread in my hands, scanning the sky for birds when I notice Kazhal sitting on her roof, which is attached to ours.

"So many birds," she says.

"They all come to my roof," I tell her and sit down.

"You love birds, don't you?"

"They love me, too."

She laughs and walks to my roof. We make small talk about the weather and the neighbours. Spring is over and schools are closed.

We begin to meet on the rooftop every evening as it gets cooler. She tells me that she hates the neighbours, the people, the city. I touch my chin, wondering if she really is Misery.

Kazhal has graduated from high school, like Azad. She is seven months older than him, which is not good because Mom says women get older sooner than men and if one gets old when her husband is still young, he will go marry a new woman.

"I love to go shopping every day, but Mom does not let me," she says. "Neighbours talk, Mom says, if I go out too much. If only I was born in Tehran, I wouldn't have these restrictions." She sighs. "I have nothing to do except help around the house, which is one thing Mom wants me to do all the time, but I get bored."

"My mom does not ask me to do any housework."

"Really? My brothers don't have to do anything. They don't even do their beds." She sighs again. "I wish I had someone to talk to."

"I have my aunt but you can talk to me."

"Really?" She smiles.

"Really," I say and hold her hands.

44

Kazhal sees her name in the newspaper, announcing that she has been admitted to a top college in Tabriz and can enjoy free education. Her father cannot allow a girl to stay in a far-away city by herself. "What is the use of a degree for a girl?" her mother keeps telling her. "At the end, a woman with a degree has to do the same chores every other woman does."

Kazhal has stopped showing up on her rooftop for our talks. I still watch people come and go, but never Azad. Had he known that Kazhal is Misery, would he still have preferred Misery to Vengeance?

Kazhal used to say that it is not good for a girl to stay single for long. I have seen several dressed-up families, unknown to me, go to her house with huge bouquets and pastry packages. Obviously, these sharp-dressed men have been asking for her hand in marriage.

No one expects me to marry, to be a housewife, or to have kids.

Leaves have yellowed and are falling over the alley. It is getting cold and I cannot stay long on the rooftop. Downstairs is too depressing. Dad is either absent or fighting with Mom over money, work, me, opium. How much does God hate me?

Azad. I had a feeling that I would see him today. I am excited to tell him that I have made friends with Kazhal and that she is Misery. Azad does not talk. He stares at the Awyar mountains and I at him. I wonder if he likes the snow on their distant peaks, if it looks like bridal lace to him too. He is silent, fully dressed in black, and has grown a beard.

"Wanna sit in my chair?" I ask.

"She's engaged to a hideous bastard," he says finally.

"Kazhal?"

"She deserved a better man. Her parents exchanged her for his money." He rubs his ear and looks down at the pebbles on the roof. I look at him.

My family is invited to Kazhal's wedding party. Almost everyone in the neighbourhood goes to see how a wealthy groom throws a wedding party. I would love to see Kazhal in a white wedding dress, her face under bridal lace. I can wear a Kurdish dress and sit still. Nothing can help with my chin, however. I stay home and Mom does not go either. As usual, she never leaves me alone at home. I wish I were Misery rather than Vengeance and could put on a beautiful wedding dress.

Azad is not accepted to a university and like all Iranian boys has to do his two years compulsory military service. "It is the only misery of being a boy," my mom says while talking to Azad's mother on the phone. It is not yet known which city he will be sent to and his parents are very anxious about it. His mother says they tried hard to get him an exemption by faking a physical problem, and then with bribes. Legally, he would not have to go if there was something wrong with his body. I wonder what it would be like if there was something wrong with his body . . . no military service . . . probably no Kazhal . . . maybe he would be involved with me. No, I want him happy, never want him to be Vengeance. If only I could enter the River of Milk and Honey for just a moment! I would wait for him for two years, even more.

☄

I have not been able to go to the roof much because of the winter cold and when I go I cannot sit calmly; these days I am restless. Each of my little birds has a mate now. Mom is busy doing New Year cleaning, washing up the whole place, curtains, carpets, cushions, everything, everywhere. I go down and search through my mom's old stuff in the basement where I am sure there will be makeup.

As I apply the wine-red lipstick, I look at myself in the broken mirror, at my huge, misshapen lips growing redder and redder. I close my eyes and see myself emerging from the river of milk and honey: light skin, small head, dark black eyes and hair, well-formed legs. I open my eyes and see my face in the mirror. I turn my head away immediately, hobble up the stairs and lie down on my belly on the rooftop. Hands under breasts, I kiss the ground. The pebbles and sand turn red. I kiss again and again. The last red I see is the blood of my lips. My tears, also, splotch the ground.

Mom calls me. Someone is at the door. Somebody wants to see me. It is not an aunt. I wipe my lips with the back of my dress and go down. Kazhal! She is pale and exhausted. Her skin and eyes do not sparkle any more. She says that mine are red and wet, as she hugs me. I can see tears welling in her eyes. Mom looks surprised at us both. Kazhal wants us to go to the roof.

She cries. Soon after her wedding, her father found out that her husband did not own the store he claimed to own, nor did he have any of the things that he had said belonged to him. Her husband's car was actually his brother's. "Why should I be a divorced woman, before I am even twenty? For which sin?" she cries. I try hard to control my tears.

They were lucky, though, to figure out his lies before the marriage was consummated. So she is still a virgin, for which they thank God. A divorce is a divorce, though, too significant of a taboo. She says she does not know if she should just not mind his lies and stay with him. "But what is the use of a penniless, lying husband?" she asks me. "But then who would marry a divorced woman? A man with two other wives?" Kazhal tells me that her husband says that he told those lies because he loves her. Her mother sneers at her for being a fool to be deceived by the man. Kazhal does not know what to do. She tells me that she actually hates him, and hates her mother for making all the decisions on her behalf and then blaming her. Sometimes she even hates herself for being so wretched and sometimes she hates all women for being such miserable creatures. I hold her hands in mine.

I Am One of Them

THE PHONE ON THE BEDSIDE table has been blaring constantly for a while now. The computer monitor has darkened but Shajaryan's traditional, mellow song comes quietly from the desk speakers. A girl in her twenties sits cross-legged on a wooden bed, wearing a pair of ear plugs; her head is bowed over a bamboo pen as she cuts its nib. Glossy papers are spread over the bed, some already blackened with Persian calligraphy. A vibration begins between the white sheets next to her legs. Then a knocking on the bedroom door, followed by a woman's voice: "Zanyar is gone, open the door now. I need to talk to you."

The girl tilts her head and keeps shaping the nib on her left index finger. Strands of her black hair have fallen across her forehead and brows; her face and chest are sweaty. There is a large portable mirror on the bed, nudging the edge of her long brown skirt. The jiggling black cell phone is now visible between the sheets near her foot. She picks up a stone from the pen case, containing black and dark blue ink bottles, to sharpen the knife, her brows drawn together. The phone rings again.

The knock becomes firmer, as does the voice. "Sana, open this door. You drive me nuts. I'll bury this wish with me in a grave to have you listen to me once in your life. Oh God! Kill me and save me from these kids."

The vibrating cell phone is touching Sana's toe now. Taking out the ear plugs, with her toe she kicks the cell off the bed, spreads her legs and runs the point of the knife along the sheets. The cell vibrates on the floor and the phone blares. After picking up a dark bamboo pen from the case, she reaches for the home phone wire and unplugs it. Sana moves her head left, strands of hair still covering her eyebrows. With a forearm, she sweeps away her hair and wipes the sweat from her brow. The lights are off and the open curtains do not let much daylight in. The cell phone begins to vibrate again on the handmade persian wool rug next to the bed. She stretches her arms overhead, turning her neck from left to right. Leaning forward over the edge of the bed, Sana picks up the jiggling cell, opens it; the screen reads, "Susan." She pulls her finger away from the red button and presses the call button.

"Sana, hello, Sana, why do you want to break up with Zanyar?" a girl's voice comes on the line. Sana does not answer. "Is that true? . . . Hello . . . Sana, are you alive? Were you sleeping?"

"No . . ." Sana shakes her head. "Not even for a second since yester—"

"I don't care if I wake you! Why don't you answer the phone or return my calls?" Susan shouts. "Zanyar came here today. Isn't he your damn dream man any more?"

Sana holds her hand on her rising breast; she closes her eyes and her chest falls.

"The principal was asking for you. I said you were sick and will be back to school tomorrow. Right?"

"I—"

"Poor Zanyar. He's freaking out. I can't believe it. What's this mess about, Sana?" Susan is talking rapidly and loudly.

Sana lays the hand with the cell down on the sheet and breathes deeply. When she holds the phone back to her ear she hears ". . . you in a few minutes."

"Nooo!" Sana almost shouts.

"Swear to God! What's wrong? Sana . . . Sana? . . . This is not like you at all."

Sana swallows, looks up and gazes into the mirror on the bed. "I am different and I can't do anything about it."

The woman knocks on the door again. "Sana, who're you talking to? God, open this door!"

"Of course! No one is a stupid-head like you are," Susan says.

Sana pinches her black shirt away from her chest and watches the air conditioner. "It's so hot."

"Swear to God! Raining fire."

Sana presses down on the corners of her eyes. "Or it's just me."

"No, it's above forty-five. Sultry," Susan explains.

"Sana, open this door. Oh God! Are you talking to yourself? Have you gone crazy, Sana? When will you let me have one peaceful day? You stress me to death!"

"She's actually putting her ear on my door." Sana's voice seems far away.

"Yeah, it's one of those days. I'm never gonna get used to this killingly hot and humid island."

"It's just me!" Sana says, her eyes on the door, her eyebrows drawing downward.

"What's that?"

Sana cradles the cell on her right ear, and scratches her slim arm, which turns red. She notices her chipped nails and bleeding fingers. "Damn!"

"What's going on with you, Sana?" Susan asks in a calm tone.

"I'm cut!" Sana rubs her bleeding finger on the blanket.

"Swear to God? A cut?"

"Cut!" She picks up the mirror by its handle. "Yeah, just a small, unimportant . . . Oh no, a small but important, celestial cut!" Sana turns the mirror backward. "I used to think all Sunni girls . . . but it's just some areas, some countries . . ."

"What? Why do you sound so far away?"

Sana turns the mirror around. "This cursed Qeshm . . . almost all Qeshmi girls and women."

"We're what? Cursed?" Susan asks.

"You're not Qeshmi!"

"Well, I'm almost Qeshmi. So, am I half-doomed?"

Sana throws the mirror down on the blanket, walks with difficulty to the curtain designed with large climbing aubergine tulips on a satin-style green fabric. "At least my feet are tingling. I'm not as numb as I thought." She picks up the curtain corners and pulls them to the wall so that not even a single light beam can enter the room.

"You gotta get some fresh air into that head of yours," Susan says, not speaking as rapidly as before but still loudly.

"Stop shrieking in my ear and giving advice, please. All right?"

"*Fine!*"

Sana turns her back to the curtain and wraps it around her waist. "Heh, I tuned on Shajaryan but then I put earplugs in my ears."

"I'm not surprised."

Sana rubs her face on the velvet tulip petals on the curtain, wrapping herself in it.

"He asks me, 'So are you a freak?'" Sana says and begins to unwrap herself. "I should've said, 'Yes I am, dear. You're getting married to a frea—' Ouch!" She's stepped on the plug of a hair dryer lying on the ground.

"What happened?" She kicks the hair dryer away.

"Sana, you'd better open the door before your father gets back. Oh God! Do you hear me?" The woman knocks. "Sana! Open this. What are you going to do? Do you know what you're doing? You make us the talk of the entire island. You're absolutely thoughtless. What will people say?"

Sana hops onto the bed and pulls up her feet to examine her toe.

"Did you cut your foot? Hands?" Susan asks.

"Cut!" Sana says under her breath. Her eyes are on the fresh blood on her toe.

"What's that?" Susan sounds irritated.

"That's a cut, my friend, I am cut like the women of African tribes, some places in Indonesia, Malaysia, some Arab countries . . ."

"Hey! Are you okay?"

"Should I be?"

"I don't understand. I mean I'm used to your craziness but I can't figure this one out. Why do you want to break up with Zanyar?"

"I would break up with my parents, too, if I could, with the whole island, as well . . . with life, probably." Sana wipes the blood with the blanket, which is already bloodstained.

"Poor Zanyar! He's totally stressed out and he says he won't go back to Kurdistan unless he makes sure you're back to your senses."

Sana reaches under the pillow and removes a framed photo. "We were having a good time last night." In the photo Sana's head is on the shoulder of a young man with a black moustache, long hair to his shoulders, and big, brown eyes. She is staring at the camera, grinning, and he is looking at her from the corners of his eyes. "Then we started talking about freaks . . . he started talking about this damn TV show he watched recently, thinking that he's telling me something en-ter-tain-ing. 'Have you ever heard about this?'

Oh, Susan." She tosses the photo away. "He hadn't even heard about it before . . . I felt like I couldn't move any more; I couldn't even swallow. My gaze was fixed on his mouth while he talked and talked to the point where I couldn't even guess what those oily lips were saying."

"What . . . are you . . . talking about?" Susan asks.

"I said, 'Hey, I am one of them.' Do you understand, Susan? I said, 'Hey Zanyar, I am one of those you haven't even heard about.' And then I laughed and he laughed. What did he laugh at? I wasn't trying to entertain him! This is not a joke. It's not."

"Shut up, Sana, now. Please tell me you're not serious! Wait, I am so confused! That can't be true!" Susan cries out.

"What do you know, Susan? You weren't born in Qeshm."

"I heard something, didn't really believe it! . . . But, you are so different from all the Qeshmi girls. Your family is the most open-minded I've come across. Your parents give you rights, freedoms. I mean . . . not lots . . . but compared to any other girl on the island . . . you have your own room, you know, you have your cell phone, your friends."

Sana doesn't answer.

"And it was stopped a while ago, no?"

Sana is motionless, holding her breath, eyes on the far end of the room where the wall cuts into the ceiling. The mellow and soothing sound of a santur becomes audible once again from the speakers.

"Isn't that true? . . . Sana!" Susan says.

"What's that?"

"Wasn't it stopped . . . many years ago?" Susan's voice seems distant.

"No, not many! Not too many, too late for me."

"Sana, I'm putting down some food here for you," the woman at the door says. "Karafs stew and rice, your favourite. Just take it in your room. I'm leaving."

"That's why everyone around me is just like me—even her!" Sana looks at the door.

"Who's 'her'?" Susan asks.

"Zanyar is away and I'm leaving, okay? Try a spoonful, at least," the woman implores.

"He and she and all the parents . . . They haven't committed a crime . . . They were just doing a sacred Sunnah . . . They're pure, innocent, kind, caring. Look how she is freaking out over me, my mom . . . Over me?" She shrugs. "Or over what people will say if they can't find a husband for their daughter! They were just making sure we won't turn into bad women . . . That we won't become whores!" Sana swallows and blinks. Her eyes are wet.

"Shut up, Sana. Now. This is your worst practical joke ever," Susan cries.

"Joke!" Sana's eyes meet the poster of Parviz Meshkatian's profile on the closed door, bending over his santur with his long grey beard. She takes out a black suitcase from under the bed, her neck leaning on her shoulder to keep the cell at her ear. She takes out a few dresses and pants with edges decorated with gold and silver strings and sequins. A santur lies under the dresses. She bends over it, opens her arms, and puts her cheek on its strings.

"Listen! Let's go for a walk by the sea." Susan's voice is deeper than before.

Sana puts away the cell and runs her fingertips on the steel strings. Then she holds the two mallets between her index and middle fingers and plucks the strings of the santur. The notes double in frequency as she plays the strings on the left.

"Stop being a fool, Sana," says the woman at the door, "Zanyar still wants you, do you understand? You're destroying your future. Think about it, no one else will want you if you break up. People will think there's something wrong with our daughter. What are you gonna do? Stay in this house till your hair turns the colour of your teeth? Don't kick your luck . . . Oh God!"

Sana stops playing, places the clothes back over the instrument, locks the suitcase and pushes it under the wooden bed. She holds the cell to her ear. "Still there?"

"Why did you stop?"

"It was out of tune."

"Tune it and play it. That might help you get back to your senses."

Sana takes the cell in her other hand. "They're just benefactors; they want the best for you. They know things that you won't understand in a hundred years. Like how you'll be a whore if you play music," Sana says as if talking to herself, sweat gleaming upon her skin.

"All right?"

"What?"

"Let's go for a walk."

"Naaah." Sana leans her elbow on the bed, seated on the carpet. The glossy papers under her elbow crinkle. "How would you— no—how was I supposed to answer that question?"

"Which question?"

"I laughed so loud that everyone in the restaurant looked at me and he got mad at me for attracting attention, and then . . . I couldn't stand it. I had to run away when he went to the washroom."

"Why?"

"I could only laugh, then. I just laughed. That's all I could do." Sana puts her arms around her knees.

"I can't believe people in Iran actually do that." Susan's voice seems to come from a distance.

Sana stands up. "My best friend finds it hard to even imagine. My fiancé, too. That's why I'm a secret freak, a hidden freak. I have to break up."

"Listen! There's no reason to freak out, though."

"You're not a freak . . . heh!"

"Swear to God! You aren't either."

Sana goes to the chair and grabs a pile of shirts, jeans, and under-wear draped over the back, throws them away and sits down. "Ha ha . . . really? You shouldn't freak out when you suddenly find out you're a freak?" Sana picks up the mirror, but puts it down without looking at it. "I must see a doctor."

"I swear to God. What kind of doctor?"

"I need a female gynecologist to tell me what the difference is . . . But I am one of them. That's what I told him last night. I said, 'Hey Zanyar, I'm one of them.' He asked, 'Have you ever heard . . .' I thought he knew, I thought his own mother and sisters were like me. I thought for him, too, it's a holy Sunnah!" Sana claws her hair, closes her eyes, bites her lip.

"Oh, Lord! Let's look it up on the internet and find some pic-tures. I'll try to ask my brother for some proxy breakers."

"Freak, freak, freak!" Sana punches the back of the mirror.

Susan is breathing quickly.

"I have to break up, finish this," Sana says, standing up. "Do you understand? I have to."

"Listen, it'd be good to talk to some doctor."

"I wish I could think clearly!"

"Swear to God, maybe it's not such a big deal!"

"The left part of my body is numb." Sana rubs her arm. Susan is quiet.

"He said the TV show said that men whose wives are like that have a higher tendency to marry a second wife or get secret lovers."

"Did Zanyar actually say that? Really say that?"

"Oh, God! You ungrateful girl, you didn't even touch it, and I entreated you. All right! Your father will be in soon and I'll tell him. You'll be in big trouble," the woman at the door says.

"This'll be an excuse, like a defect he can use to justify any unhappiness in our life . . . I must finish this."

"Listen! Men usually cheat when they think they cannot satisfy the woman. You can just fake it. Not that they care about how a woman feels. They're mostly concerned about themselves. So just fool him."

"And myself as well?"

"Ah! Maybe it's not such a big deal. You know what I mean?"

"Isn't he the one you wanted so bad, you wayward girl? Didn't your father and I tell you a million times to forget about *Sarhadi* men? You didn't want Qeshmi men. Now you have to stick to your choice. There's no way I'd let you shame us." The knocks on the door are firmer than ever.

Frowning, Sana claws at her skirt, lifts the fabric up in her fist and stares at it. "When they do that to boys, they celebrate it and decorate the house with balloons and stuff, sacrifice some kind of animal . . . and yes, they help him medically . . . but they submit the little girls to an old woman with a razor and then . . . just when the girl grows up . . ." She grinds her teeth.

"Swear to God, maybe doctors can do something about it."

"I used to think it was ordinary . . . normal! No big deal, but . . ." She goes to the bed and picks up the knife. "I couldn't stay there any more. He wasn't at that table, in front of me, and I could see that everyone in the restaurant was staring at me, I felt I was a circus freak, so I grabbed my purse and ran here."

"Listen, just don't let this run you down. Keep your confidence and make sure . . . Listen, it has nothing to do with who you are as a person."

Sana laughs and then goes to lie down on the bed, head on a glossy paper covered with Persian calligraphy.

"I'm not even a complete human," Sana says, picking up the knife.

"Sana, Oh God! Sana! Your father is back and he is going to talk to you," the woman at the door says.

"Tell my benefactors to celebrate their honour," Sana says under her breath, her eyes on the edge of the knife. "My purity, my chastity!"

Sana's cell beeps and the line goes dead with a click. She throws it back onto the floor. Sana lies on the bed, the glossy papers crinkling under her, the woman knocking, a man's voice calling her name at the door. The music ends and everything turns silent for a moment, her finger touching the tip of the knife, her dark, stern eyes looking right and left.

Glass Slippers

"SOMEONE'S COMING!"

"Just one?"

"Uh-huh!"

"Alone?"

"Yes."

"Is it Yusuf?"

"A woman."

Something falls inside you. You put your hand on your sister's back, and wait for her to step down; but she raises herself higher, on tip-toes. Staring at Sara's head, turned away from you, you want to ask her what else she sees, but your tongue, dry and stuck to the roof of your mouth, fails to move. Sara has her head pressed against the thin steel bars of the only window in the electronics shop storeroom. She raises her chin and peers through. Your place is three houses down from here, off the narrow alley into which Sara is peering. This block is honeycombed with dilapidated houses and a few apartments.

"Sara." You manage to say her name, but in a voice barely recognizable as your own.

"Shhh!"

You draw back your hand from her back. Your fingers feel cold and a bit tingly.

"Hide your head!" Sara turns back quickly and you put your hand on her back.

She sits on an old radio, pulling your sleeve to sit you down on something as well, something that makes a harsh creaking sound in the room's clutter of electronic debris. It might have been a working TV once. You stare at her lips nervously, bidding them to tell you what the woman who passed through the alley looked like. Her eyes are inattentive, and she says nothing.

But who can move in this cramped room? When you breathe, your breath hits some electronic thing and makes an annoying crackling sound. Perhaps Yusuf is home and has called this woman over? He must have called her from his store. You imagine her with a large body; Yusuf likes big women. You feel the black chador that chastely covers your petite body, and gingerly slide a hand towards your small breasts—but you are in shape, your belly is flat, your face is cute, that's what everyone says. There is the clack of high heels as her footsteps pass by the window, and you look down at your scuffed running shoes. From today on, you vow to be more feminine.

"Okay." Sara steps up on the crate again and pushes her face against the bars. The electronic objects rattle against each other, disturbing your nerves further.

"What's she like?" you ask hesitantly.

"Horrible!" Sara turns and frowns for you.

"Let me see," you reply, gaining courage.

"Wait!"

"Please, Sara!" Your insides are churning. She peers intently out the window. "Sara, please."

"Shhh! She's going into your house now," she murmurs.

You get up and want to push her aside. You need to see with your own eyes, for yourself. Sara is trying to squeeze more of her head through the rods and you want to scream at her to get out of your way.

"She didn't," Sara says surprisingly and turns back towards you, shaking her head. "She didn't go to your house."

You clasp hands together and take a step forward eagerly. "What's she doing?"

"She walked out of the alley," Sara says, peering through the bars again.

"You sure?"

"Uh-huh."

"Was she pretty?" you ask shyly, blood running into your face.

"Ha ha . . . so?"

You shrug to yourself, embarrassed. "Just . . . watch for her. She might return," you say, pretending that you can handle the situation and that you are not relieved because she simply passed by your door without knocking.

"Obviously she's not from around here, maybe not from Qom even. And she can't be on a pilgrimage. What's she doing in this neighbourhood?" Sara pulls herself up to the window again.

"Why? What was she wearing?"

"Dressed like a classy whore! Jeans, a short manteau, a thin head-scarf, highlighted hair, light purple makeup . . ." Sara is spitting out these words.

Is she visiting some other poor woman's husband? You swallow, frozen behind Sara, unable to stand or sit down. The room is dark except for the beam of light from the tiny window. The crackling of the junk at your feet and against your hips is bothersome and you try not to move, not even to breathe. You wonder why the old man has gathered so much rubbish. Why on earth do human beings collect garbage? What is the difference between a storage closet and a trash room?

Your father's basement was like this. Your mother used to put every unnecessary thing in the basement that smelled sour and damp. But you liked the smell. The ceiling was not cobwebbed like this one. It was a good place to hide as well, when your father or one of your seven brothers was not in a good mood. Going through the boxes every now and then, finding old forgotten textbooks, notebooks, clothes, and toys used to be one of your hobbies.

The day Yusuf and his family came to your house to ask for your hand in marriage you hid with Sara in the basement to spy on them as they passed through the yard. You were scared to death: if you did not like the boy—and Sara already did not—who would dare protest your father's and brothers' choice? Your father would rather see you dead than reject his landlord's son.

That day you and your sister put gunny sacks over your heads and went to peer out of the corner of the broken window in the basement. You did the same when Morteza came to ask for Sara's hand, although Sara did not let Morteza meet you until her wedding day because she was concerned that her fiancé might change his mind and ask for the younger daughter's hand. When Yusuf and his family passed through the yard, Sara did not leave the broken window and did not let you see. You pleaded with Sara, but she did not budge from the window. You implored her to talk about him at least. All she said was, "He is so different from Morteza."

It was love, like in the movies, at first sight. You fell for Yusuf's eyes, the blackest eyes. You married without extravagant ceremony and then lived in an old house Yusuf's father had rented to his son. Yusuf still works in the same barber shop next to his father's store where your father is a retailer. When Yusuf is around, you rarely hear his footsteps or voice. Yusuf has never yelled at you or laid a hand on you, has never bullied you. He knows poetry by heart, cares for sparrows, feels pity for the fish imprisoned in the small pond of the yard, and loves flowers. You love him.

"Did you tell him you'd return soon?" Sara asks.

You stare at the wrinkles drawing down the corners of her mouth.

"Hey!" she says.

"He didn't ask. I didn't say."

"He sure doesn't waste any time." She tilts her head, hand under chin. Her scarf and manteau are dusty.

"Aren't you tired?" you hear yourself asking.

"Wait a bit. They'll come, eventually."

The air tastes stale. You swallow. "Perhaps he won't."

"They will, both of them, but not together, one by one."

You wipe the dust off the back of her manteau as she struggles to push her head back between the window bars.

"He might be concerned about the neighbours," you say.

The crate topples and Sara immediately steps off, spins around, and almost loses her balance. You hold her arm. Sara pauses for a moment, juts her head forward, and raises an eyebrow: "Are you suggesting they might've gone somewhere else?"

"No!"

"What?" she seems irritated.

"Nothing! I just thought he might not . . . maybe he doesn't ·want to have her in there . . . our house." You have no idea how that sentence jumped out of you, the last two words pronounced so quietly you could barely hear yourself. Why is your voice so high, like a mouse's?

"How can you be such a bloody fool? If he didn't like to have her in the house, he wouldn't keep the lady's lipstick and blue bra in the closet!"

Oh, the bra was padded but not very big; it could have been yours if it was new, if you didn't smell another woman on it. You turn towards the dark centre of the storeroom. Time feels mercilessly slow. "Would you give me another of your painkillers?" You are quite sure this headache will never leave. She takes her bag from her shoulder and hands it to you. Grabbing two pills, you swallow them reluctantly. From the window, above Sara's head, you notice the edge of a new building. You had just glimpsed someone looking your way, from the fifth floor. You even saw the corner of a skirt, you think. The blue curtain moves aside again: blue, his favourite colour. He bought you that silk dress last month. Yusuf does have exquisite taste. He bought a pair of glass high-heel slippers. "For my Cinderella," he said tenderly. He told you he had been thinking of saving up for the dress and slippers for over three months. It was his birthday and you had baked him a cake.

"I should've bought you something, Yusuf, not you me," you said, blushing.

And you were over the moon until you stupidly told your sister about what you found in the closet between his underwear. Oh, he combed your hair and asked you not to cut it short any more, and then he asked you to put blue colouring in your hair. Mother hates it; that's why you tie your headscarf tight in front of everyone, even women. Well, you have a husband now: when he tells you to colour your hair, you obey him, and your family has no right to comment on that, nor does anyone else. But Yusuf entreated you not to let anybody, especially your brothers, know because they would say Yusuf is not man enough to forbid his wife to make herself up like a whore. So you pleaded with your mother not to tell your brothers.

"What day is it today?" Sara asks, fingering her lower lip.

"I don't . . . know."

Sara puts an old, big, broken vacuum under her feet and steps up on it. You want her to talk. You hate the silence. As you look around at the pile of electronics in the darkness your heart palpitates. What day is it? You have difficulty remembering which year you are in. When did he buy you the blue dress? The glass slippers? He styled your hair gently, then asked you to wear makeup. He told you to use an eye shadow to complement the dress. Then he fetched blue mascara. He said the eye shadow was very light and coloured your eyelids, and then added some more colour to your eyelashes. You noticed that the mascara case was not new but you didn't mention it. The salesman might have deceived him. Never having seen him so excited, you swooned under his delicate hands as they skilfully painted your face. You felt for the first time that he cherished you. Fixed on his lips you coyly wet your own with the tip of your tongue, and leaned in for a long kiss. He disappointed you but continued to look at you and to say how beautiful you were, even prettier than on your wedding day. He hated that red makeup; only then you understood why he was so upset on the day of your wedding.

"Sahar!" Sara turns to you, deep in thought. "Maybe they went into the house before we got inside the storeroom."

"In that short time?"

"Yes."

You go numb.

"You have the keys?"

You nod.

"Give them to me."

You take the keys from your bag, trying to keep your hands steady.

"Follow me," she says.

Sara pushes through the broken samovars, telephones, and other junk. Your chador gets stuck to the wire of an old hair dryer, and for a moment holds you back. Sara looks at you, hands on hips, and shakes her head. You tug the chador, tearing it. Once out of the storeroom and in the store, you smile and nod your head to thank the old, deaf man fixing a TV. He smiles and you see a golden tooth in the left corner of his mouth.

Sara runs to your house and you follow her. At the gate, you pause and look at each other, breathing heavily. You lean on the wall and pray that no one will pass through the alley just then. Sara opens the door quietly. Your feet weigh a ton, they hardly move. Loud music is the first thing you notice as you enter the yard. The music could be coming from one of the neighbours, but it is not hard to recognize his favourite love song, "Dance, beautiful."

"There you go," your sister smirks, walking slowly alongside the wall and you quietly follow behind her. Sara grasps the knob of the main door and you expect it to be locked. It is not.

The trembling has spread to every part of your body. Together, you pass through the front corridor and reach the living room door. You want to open it right away, but your shaking prevents you. Even Sara looks pale and the loud music beats in your head. Sara is swearing under her breath. Even at that moment, when you are about to be certain that Yusuf has actually wronged you, her swearing at him is intolerable. You feel miserable. "I'd rather my man lay a hand on me than cheat," Sara cries.

You look at Sara at the threshold of the doorway, her big mouth and the wrinkles around it; she could swallow a man in a second. You go a step forward, grasp the door handle, not wanting to turn around and see her face any more. It seems like no one is speaking inside; maybe he is home alone, maybe he simply did not feel good enough to go to work. Finally, you open the door but cannot move forward—Sara pushes you in.

There is a woman in the room in your blue dress and glass slippers. She has long blue hair and is dancing in front of the large mirror in the living room. The woman turns to you; her heavy, repulsive makeup makes her look like a hooker even though her face is under some tulle. She seems familiar, but you fail to recognize her, you cannot see clearly. Sara steps forward, mouth open.

The woman takes the blue wig off and looks down. Sara screams. You do not realize what is going on and you look at Sara and hear her saying things that you don't understand. The woman takes off your glass slippers, which are too small for her feet. You look into those familiar, the blackest eyes and rub your own.

Silk Shawl

FURTIVE SHADOWS DANCED IN THE top-floor windows of the building I was headed for. Distant music attracted my attention as I got out of the car. I looked around to make sure there were no police cruisers around to notice my red heels. Amir was by the door, fixing his white-striped blue tie. I tucked loose strands of hair under my headscarf and wondered how he dared wear the tie I had presented to him on our anniversary.

I walked straight to the elevator and pressed "24." Amir jumped in just as the elevator door closed.

"Hello, hello. Come in." Aria had already opened the door of the apartment as we reached his floor. The two men hugged.

"How are you doing?" Amir asked.

"Never been better!" said Aria, putting a hand on Amir's shoulder as he turned to greet me. He looked massive, big as a bull with a beer belly. "Happy Birthday," I said.

Mona came to us. We repeated the usual greetings, hugged and touched cheeks, like we were kissing.

There were lots of people inside that I did not know. On the left as I entered Aria and Mona's apartment, there was a huge table with foods neatly displayed on it: white rice with zereshk, saffron, and cinnamon; stews of green ghorme with dried lemons and meats; fesenjoon made of ground nuts, pomegranate sauce and chicken; cutlets, salads, and deserts. Dozens of gold-rimmed plates had been stacked on the table, with spoons, forks, and knives arranged alongside rows of glasses turned over, and tissues under each. It seemed as though everything on that table had been measured out with a ruler.

Amir sat on the very first chair in the living room on the right, and I walked straight ahead and entered the bedroom. I changed and went to the mirror. In came Mona with blossoming cheeks. "I bet you could hear the music from outside, couldn't you?" she asked.

"Not that loud, but the shadows on the windows are dangerous," I said, still staring in disbelief at the mirror.

She drew her eyes together, "Look at you!" She came closer. "Where did you get this?"

"The colour's blinding me," I said.

"No, it's a beautiful red. Spin."

I turned a little, saying, "Everything is so weird lately. I get a headache as soon as I see anything red. Yesterday we were in the Anahita Restaurant." I turned a little more. "Have you been there? Tables, walls, windows, everything's red. I couldn't stand it there. I got a horrible headache!"

"Did you say you saw shadows? Oh, I definitely don't want anything to ruin my night," she said, all excited.

"Take it easy! One night isn't a thousand nights. And you could always send them away with a bottle and some cash."

"What a soft fabric." She touched my dress. "I've never seen a dress like this."

"Just put a blanket over the window. That's what everyone does these days."

"Hopefully they haven't already started searching houses with blankets over their windows."

"You bet."

"I bet this is not made in Iran."

"America," I said.

"Oh . . . your aunt's gift? Isn't it?" Mona emphasized the "oh" like she had just solved a riddle.

I nodded.

"Is she still here?"

"No. Left." I turned to the mirror. "Twenty-six days ago."

"You never mentioned that to me! Never mind, you've been pretty insane lately." Still staring at my dress, Mona added, "Why did you show up so late?"

I shrugged. "Didn't feel like partying."

She let go of my dress. "What? Are you crazy? You nearly killed me, insisting that I throw this party!"

I didn't reply.

"Hurry up! We're serving dinner," she said as she left the room.

"Okay."

"You look incredible!" Mona's head popped in through the door again just to say that.

I took my red silk shawl out of my bag and laid it across my bare shoulders. The woman in the mirror had red lips and fake long red nails. All that red made me dizzy. When I looked again, I noticed the wrinkled eyes and forehead. Ugly, ugly!

Three girls came in, chatting rapidly. I took Aria's present out of my bag, left the bedroom, and put the gift where everyone else had put theirs. The guests had queued to grab food, which now smelled terrible to me. I picked up some salad and walked towards Aria and Amir. They were sitting side by side, whispering and laughing. I didn't doubt that Aria had some new dirty joke, one of those you couldn't say to just anyone. Amir's plate was on the chair beside him. I sat by Aria and patted him on the back. "Let me hear."

"Amir will tell you later," he said and turned to him again.

Amir was staring at my dress, but that son of a bitch ignored my new look. I took some salad with my fork. Awfully bitter. I wanted to throw it up. Was it the cucumber? I shot the plate under my chair.

Most of the chairs in the living room were empty. It was less crowded than I had imagined. I recognized only Azita, Mona's cousin, on my right. There were five chairs between us, four of them not taken. The man beside her must be her new husband. I remembered Mona had told me about him. Azita and I smiled and nodded in greeting.

Next to Azita and her man sat a whispering and giggling couple. Both had white suits on. The girl's pants were slit right to her knees. So what? Stupid girl, you could wear short pants. Choose. Long or short? Come to terms with yourself. Look at the male clown whispering in his wife's ear and grinning, like there have been no other lovers on the earth but them. Look! They're staring at me. Well, keep staring until you go blind.

Right across from me was the birthday boy's table with lots of snacks—chocolates, chips, biscuits, candies—and under it plenty of gifts. Amidst the furniture were balloons of different colours. A tall young man with long black hair picked one up. He was in a gray shirt and a pair of jeans—torn ones, the current fashion. Had he appeared in public in those pants, they would have arrested him in a second. He must have changed here, too. Young men carrying bags of clothing to change at parties! Jailed just for carrying those.

It would be awesome if I could hide his public pants. Oh, why was I so evil!

The young man made his way over to three people sitting close to the table. They tried to grab the balloon, but he held it away. A fat one jumped onto his back and grasped it. The other two were laughing and shouting, "Run, Hamid!" The fat boy ran with the balloon into the bedroom where the girls were changing and the tall one in torn pants followed him. I heard their laughs and the girls' screams and I stood up.

Once I got to the bedroom door, I leaned against the wall, held a cigarette between my fingers and asked for a light, when the boys came out of the room laughing loudly. Both offered their lighters. I was scared by the way the taller one looked at me, so I took the fat one's. "I am Hamid," he said, "very pleased to meet you."

"His name is Pumpkin," the tall one said.

"And this is the Tower," said the fat one, receiving a swat.

Damn them both. They were eating me with their eyes.

"Nice to meet you, Pumpkin and Tower." I scratched the back of my ear with my cigarette hand.

The two girls stepped out of the bedroom. Pumpkin followed them with his gaze. I left once I saw Amir coming rapidly towards me, frowning, head tilted, hand covering mouth.

"Noushin, Noushin," Amir's voice louder the second time.

I extinguished the cigarette in the washroom. The red hag in the washroom mirror looked like those on western satellite channels.

Aria was laughing when I returned to him and Amir, who was seated once again.

"Done dirty joking?" I quipped.

Amir, his forehead wrinkled, was looking at his feet.

"You are about to enter the fourth decade of your life," I said. "Grow up, Aria."

"I'm not planning on doing so!" Aria winked at me and left his seat.

I felt a cold sweat mounting my back and shoulders.

"Noushin!" Amir's voice startled me. I didn't look at him but I could imagine his face, his pink cheeks. I remembered how he blushed when talking to girls, which made me think he was chaste. His self-righteous mother never let him talk to any girl, even to his cousins.

"Noushin!"

I was staring fixedly at the chandelier.

"What is it with this dress and such behaviour? Cigarette? You? Are you haunted? When did you start smoking?" I could see him from the corners of my eyes; he was looking at me.

"Twenty-six days ago, sir," I said.

"What? How? Why?" He came and stood next to me.

I got up and went to Azita, who was wearing a dark green shirt and skirt. Green used to be my favourite colour but this time it reminded me of sludge and squalor. I couldn't help but see Azita on a dirty, smelly morass with algae on it.

Azita kissed me. "I'm surprised to see how much you've changed!" she said.

"Who's changed?" Then I remembered that she had seen me at Aria's wedding. I was newly wed at that time and wore the hijab. "Well, everything has changed, everyone; life has changed."

"You look so different, dear, your eyes particularly. And you look thin and pale." Azita was giving me a pitiful look.

"Oh! This face?" I put my hands under my eyes. "Well . . . nothing important."

"You look gorgeous; don't get me wrong and the dress suits you so well. Are you on a diet?" Azita asked.

"A serious one!" I smirked.

"Your husband hasn't changed at all." She looked at Amir.

"Men change more than us, though not in appearance," I said under my breath and crossed one leg over the other.

"Pardon?"

"Nothing." I bit the corner of my lip.

"Financial problems are not just yours, dear. We're all in the same boat. Did Mona tell you about my tragedy? I sold my house to buy another and now I have to rent because in just one week the price of the house I wanted to buy went up and I could no longer afford it."

"That's not a real tragedy, but yeah it's ridiculous. I'm sorry to hear that."

"What do you mean it's not a real tragedy? My money is losing its value every minute."

"Well, the United States will threaten to attack and then houses will be cheap again, trust me. And it's not tragedy, because inflation is something we can get used to; betrayal and oppression are not." I looked down. I needed a corner alone to immerse myself in my own thoughts.

"Oh, we are. It's been centuries," Azita said and I felt she was examining me head to toe, reading me.

"Persians speak out more than any other people who live under totalitarianism, Azita." I turned to her after I don't know how long; her look was diverted towards Amir.

"He is still fasting every Thursday, isn't he?" Azita asked.

"Who? Him?" I asked without really looking at Amir. "Nah. Never. I mean, not any more. It's been a long time."

"Come on!" Mona appeared out of nowhere and dragged my hands.

"Oh! I can't dance."

"Yeah, right!"

"I haven't danced in ages, believe me." Pumpkin was dancing with one of the girls I had seen in the bedroom. "Ask your cousin to dance."

Mona winked at her cousin. Azita gave her small purse to the man next to her and got up. I noticed that she had still not introduced the man to anyone in our company. So the man was not official.

I stood there motionless, feeling everyone's eyes on me. The shawl could drop off my chest and shoulders at any moment. I sat down. Mona frowned, interpreting my refusal to dance as disrespectful to her party, I supposed. I felt embarrassed enough to get up but went to the kitchen instead, taking short steps so that my skirt wouldn't creep any higher.

Different kinds of soft drink were available on the kitchen table. Aria was sitting there with a water bottle containing a yellow liquid. I put a hand on my hip, dropped a shoulder and flicked my hair, just as I had rehearsed. He put the bottle on the table and looked at me.

"Are you having fun?" He took an almond.

I looked at him and back at the kitchen door behind me. "Everything's perfect," I said. "Except that there's no one to dance for." I tilted my head and looked straight into his dark brown eyes.

"I'll be there soon." He smiled.

I pointed awkwardly towards the door. "Please."

He choked his drink and walked towards me, wiping his mouth on his sleeve. I tightened my shawl around my shoulder.

"In Aria's honour!" I raised my hands and clapped as we entered the living room. Everybody turned, applauded, and whistled. Mona started dancing with Aria.

I returned to the kitchen, looked at the table, and picked one of the glasses which had two pieces of ice in it. I crumpled into a seat and stared at the chador under the table that was supposed to hide the liquor bottles. I used to hate alcohol and its smell.

I put the glass down and looked at the nakedness of my arms, then I started pushing my skirt down and stockings up. But it was worth it, it was worth it, I said to myself. In the past month I had forgotten how to live. All that I'd done was watch the night's movie, which I had filmed on my camera, and talk to myself. I wouldn't have gone mad if, at least, I hadn't lost my job. Amir had tried to calm me. He kept asking what was wrong. "Nothing," I would always answer. He even called my mother: "Your daughter is not talking to me." He begged me to see a doctor. I refused.

My eyes roamed over the kitchen wall hoping to kick Amir out of my mind for a second. Was that painting on the glazed tile there before? All those hands reaching in the sky to catch hold of a scale! I remembered where I first saw this painting. It was in the coffee shop where Amir took me a couple of weeks ago, the same place we first met. We had gone there only on special occasions thus far. He had bought me white roses. He said, out of nowhere: "Forgive me." I asked why he wanted me to forgive him.

"Haven't you heard the latest news from the Persian Gulf?"

"So?" I stared at the painting that, among all the pictures on the brick wall of the coffee shop, was the one that most attracted my attention.

"There might be a war, any moment. We will be just like the Iraqi people." He stirred his cappuccino.

"Did the US tell you they're going to attack?" I asked.

"People are leaving the country. At any moment, even right now as we're sitting here, a bomb could kill us." He was still looking into his cup.

"Really?" I folded my arms on the table.

"Uhum." He sipped his drink.

"Then, I wish it would, very soon!" I leaned back on my chair as the attractive young waitress passed, carrying two ice creams on a tray.

"I'm serious. Or we may die in an earthquake, like the one in Bam." He put down his cup. "Nobody will rescue us, and even if we do get out of the destruction, we'll die of starvation."

I folded my arms again on the table and buried my head in them.

"Forgive me if I've upset you unintentionally," he said.

"If?" I looked into his eyes, chin on forearm.

"I . . . can't think of anything to say." He played with a tissue.

"You can't remember if you've hurt me or not, unintentionally?"

"I think I haven't done anything intentionally." He wiped his mouth.

"So, why are you asking for forgiveness, if you've never hurt me intentionally? How do you distinguish intentional from unintentional?" My hands grasped the edge of the table.

"I just said that . . . you know, because . . . war . . ." Amir abruptly stood up and went to the bathroom.

"May I have the honour of dancing with you, my lady?" Tower was in the kitchen, bending over the other end of the table, his palms pressing the tabletop.

I took my hands out of my hair and covered my chest. "No!" I cried and walked straight out of the kitchen. How long had he been standing there? Was I talking to myself loudly?

In the living room, men and women were wriggling around. I stayed in a corner and leaned my head against the wall. Pumpkin was crawling towards a new girl in a mini skirt. Finally, someone's skirt shorter than mine! How long was I in that kitchen by myself? My heart was still beating fast.

Amir was where I had seen him last, seated, and the male friend of Azita's was talking to him. Amir stood up abruptly, interrupted him and walked towards me. I thought he would pull my hair and draw me out of the party. I went right away to Mona and Aria and started moving my hands and body on the dance floor.

The happy giggling couple in their white shrouds were dancing, the woman staring at her husband and he looking down. I pitied her, her and her temporary happiness.

Somebody jostled me. It was Amir. I stepped back immediately; the touch of his body still disgusted me. I wriggled and over the music I could hear my heart beat. Aria went to Amir and began to dance with him. Not to make him feel left alone? I danced with Mona.

"Come on, dance with us you ladies," Aria said. I turned to him and acted just as I had rehearsed. Every detail of that movie was alive in my mind. Aria started to dance with me. Amir looked pale. My shawl fell off. Aria was absorbed with me and Amir was blushing. Did I blush much, that night? Probably not. Just like Mona, I was guileless, cheerful, and assured. But Mona's naïve face made me turn away from her. Amir was still pale but smiling at Mona, trying to dance in front of her.

A bead of sweat dropped from the corner of my eyebrow to my cheek. I had been dancing like crazy with no sense of the passage of time. Aria went to the kitchen and I followed him.

In the kitchen, I picked up an empty glass and sat next to him. I felt like I was on fire, so I took a few pieces of ice and then I picked up some more. I grabbed a bottle from under the chador beneath the table. The label read Single Malt Scotch. Aria was gazing at me without blinking. All I wanted was to have Amir enter the kitchen right then. I took the glass to my lips, watching the ice in the glass. I couldn't think of a word to start a conversation . . . all I could see was the red print of my lipstick on the glass. I offered Aria the glass and tried hard to be able to look into his eyes. His eyes had turned the colour of my dress. I unscrewed the lid, got up, ran to the fridge and poured myself some water. Aria burst into loud laughter, which made my knees tremble. Amir came in right then. I left the kitchen and went to the bedroom where I sat on the bed and held my knees in my arms.

I'm not sure if Amir's brain was able to analyze that scene; mine wasn't. Amir knew that I had rejected Aria's proposal four years ago, because I hated his drinking although everything else about him I liked. Nobody could ever guess I would end up marrying Amir, a person who seemed to be my opposite in every aspect. I had mentioned to my friends and family that I would prefer a husband who spent his time praying rather than dancing at parties. They made fun of me. What made me think a religious family would not have to deal with the very same issues as my own? Most of his relatives considered our "non-Islamic" wedding offensive and mine hated the boring, "retarded" party. I didn't put on my dream wedding dress out of respect for him and his family. His mother and sisters ended up telling him that they were too embarrassed by me—not wearing a veil on my wedding day and having music—to invite their friends and colleagues. Marriage isolated me, and Amir became my everyone.

When my aunt realized that it was our third anniversary, she asked to see our wedding pictures.

"Ugh! How do you stand these frogs?" Fakhri said, who should be called Ferri since she's an American citizen, looking at the photos of my sisters-in-law.

I stole a look at Amir. My aunt laughed.

"What's so funny about my sisters?" Amir asked.

"Come. Sit here," my aunt held his hands. "I have never met people like this in real life and I thought they existed only on CNN's made-up documentaries of Iran."

"What're you talking about?" Amir asked.

"Look at these faces with veils and covers. I mean, what is it they are trying to hide? Americans think that's what all Iranian women are like."

Amir didn't mention that he respected women who wore the hijab, nor that he never shook hands with women.

"Their ignorance is not our responsibility and those people do live in Iran and other parts of the world even though we might not come across them very often," I said, turning on the TV to change the topic.

"Seriously? You watch Islamic Republic TV? Phooey, can't believe it!" Ferri flipped the pages of the album.

"Well, these absurd channels are funnier. Also, 'they' are too strict on satellite these days. Jail and ticket for those who dare watch non-Islamic Republic channels. We're not looking for trouble. Right, Amir?" I looked at Amir who was leaning over the album so intently that it was as if he were seeing his own wedding photo album for the first time. Amir's right hand covered his mouth, his very typical gesture, while talking and blushing at the same time.

"You're too damn hot, groom," Ferri said, in English, and I noticed that she barely had a Farsi accent. Amir laughed and made up justifications for his poses and expressions in each picture. They never mentioned the bride once in their conversation!

I turned back to the TV. A reporter was interviewing some boys.

"It is our absolute right to study peacefully at the university, but we can't when we see these girls in tight manteaus," one of the boys said, whose white shirt lay untucked over his green pants.

Another teenager, sprouting facial hair, pushed the others aside to get in front of the camera and said, "It's our religious and moral responsibility to fight against unveilism. Well, Imam Khomeini said that . . . that . . . that if nudity means civilization, then animals are the most civilized. God is great!"

I flipped through the four channels. As usual, three of them featured blathering mullahs, and the last, football. I turned off the TV.

"Amir!" I said, loud enough. "What's that black plastic called that is put on the corner of donkeys' eyes?"

"What?"

"So that donkeys don't see the grass on either side and only move straight ahead," I said.

"Okay," he said, his head bent over the album.

"What's that called?"

"I don't know." He still didn't look up at me.

"Look at this one! You look like you don't even know how to hold a woman." Ferri laughed and patted Amir's arm. They must be talking about that one picture where Amir and I pretended to dance.

Amir blushed.

"Well," I said, "I was thinking that these boys can wear them. Then they might be able to study. Do you think that's enough or do you think even hearing a woman's footstep would unsettle their peace?"

Amir gave me a weird look that I had never seen before. "This is your attitude. You deserve whatever happens to you." He left the room.

"What?" I gaped.

I lifted my head from between my knees and peered through the darkness of Mona's bedroom. I remembered my aunt bursting into laughter again and I laughed, too. What had I laughed at? All I could remember was how excited I was to see Ferri, after fifteen years, the dear aunt whom I loved so much. Her departure from the country was my first experience of depression, at eleven. I remembered wearing her red-framed glasses at three and asking everyone, "Who am I now?"

Applause and hurrahs. My back hurt from bending for so long. I found it too hard to breathe in the horrifying loneliness of the cold, dark room. My feet were tingling when I walked back into the living room. Mona was bringing a cake, a white house with green roof and windows. The guests sang *tavalodet mobarak*, and Aria blew out all of the candles with one puff. I sat down on the first chair that I reached.

"We have to celebrate your anniversary!" Ferri said that night. Then she baked a cake, put on this red dress of hers, and the three of us danced. Certainly, she had intentionally perfumed her dress and left it there. I felt nauseous remembering that perfume smell. Or, perhaps, Amir had stolen it from her suitcase to remember her by. Oh how my aunt teased Amir about his amateurish dancing style.

"I'm a pro now. I didn't even know how to clap when I got married," Amir said, clownishly obeying everything she told him to do.

She put her hand on his hip. "Put your right foot back, left foot here. Now move your hips like this. Left foot doesn't move. Move your right one back and forth, back and forth. One, two, three. One, two, three." I was filming and laughing, laughing at Amir's awkwardness, enjoying my aunt's power over him. And I didn't see more. Has there ever been a blind camera person?

Aria held Mona's hand and they cut a piece of cake together. I went to help. With that sharp knife, I cut the cake so smoothly. I imagined cutting a throat with every stroke. I put each piece on a gold-rimmed plate. Aria handed plates to the guests and Azita brought some tea.

"Do you need help?" Amir asked Mona, who was handing some new plates to me.

"Thanks. Noushin is helping me out."

Amir grinned and walked towards the kitchen in hesitant steps. Aria sat beside me. I went back to the joy of cutting, felt the weight of a gaze and looked up. Tower with his torn pants, was staring at me. At once, I realized that my shawl had thoroughly slid down. I put it back on my shoulders and left my seat. As I passed him, I glanced up, wishing to spit into his dirty eyes. I could pluck all the men's eyes, especially Amir's as he stared at Ferri in her turned-down collar shirt. We had begun to play cards, Ferri and Amir having set aside the album and the dancing lesson. Every time she put down a card, we could see her chest down to her navel. I stole some looks at Amir. He was looking down, and I blamed myself for my thought. Right then, my mother called to invite us for dinner. I was on the phone when I happened to see him staring at her breast, blushing, holding his hand on his mouth.

No, I wasn't here to just sit and mope in a corner.

I sat next to Aria and started to help open his birthday presents. Mona sat next to me on the couch for two. I announced what each guest had brought. Aria was making jokes about the gifts and Mona was politely thanking the guests. I left my own present for the end.

"And this is specifically to dear Aria from me," I said loudly and saw Amir leaning against the door of the kitchen. I didn't mention his name; I pretended he didn't exist and everyone forgot about him. I told Aria I wouldn't open the gift until he could guess what was inside.

"A car? A house? A plane?" he asked, trying to be funny.

Amir stumbled forward and stared at Aria and I tried to laugh, to forget that I hated the smells of perfume and perspiration on Aria's huge body, that his laughter sounded like barking. I could feel the gaze of that bastard Tower who disgusted me along with every other object in my mind. I hated Amir standing there like a corpse. He never used to let me be more than a step away from him.

I put my hands on Aria's eyes and asked him to open the gift with his eyes closed. Amir was chewing his nails. Aria opened it slowly, and every second I despised my hands even more. Aria unwrapped the present and touched the frame of the picture. "Dear God, Noushin! No way," he said as he put his hand on my leg.

Mona was walking around making sure that the party was going on well. I took my hands from his eyes and slipped one under his that was placed on my leg.

"Yes way," I grinned.

Amir was the one who had made me reach that stage in my life. I would be able to forgive him only when I was as guilty as he was. I was ready to sell my soul to destroy his. Then I would be the one walking around asking, "Hey darling, what's wrong? Go see a doctor."

Aria touched the face of the girl in the picture who was sitting by the river washing a red apple in the water. "How did I know it's the same picture?" he asked, very excited.

"Well, because you know!" I said, and he kissed my cheek. I closed my eyes.

"It's the most wonderful painting in the world, isn't it?" he asked.

"I suppose!" I opened my eyes and tried to take a deep breath. Aria was still staring at me. I remembered his face four years ago when he told me how he had grown a habit of going to the coffee shop, sitting in front of the painting and thinking that he was having tea with the girl in the picture whom he believed would offer him an apple one day. But the look of adoration wasn't in his eyes any more. He looked like a cow to me at that moment, with dead drunk eyes.

"So, you never told me what in that girl looks like me," I said.

Mona was standing by us now, putting all the gifts into a bag.

"Just look at that stunning innocence," he said, pointing at the girl's face reflected in the limpid water.

I couldn't look into his eyes. He was sober. I was the one who was out of it. I walked fast to the bedroom and made sure to avoid the mirror.

Hands on the back of my head, I sat on the edge of the bed and clawed at my hair. "Innocence?" A lump in my throat. I didn't want to think, didn't want to know. All my senses were numb, so was my mind.

I was eleven when you fought for your rights, auntie. You said you could neither forgive your husband, nor stay in this country. You left, and I cried for losing you. You said you would return to visit me and you did. I wish you hadn't. I still hear you saying that in order to understand, one doesn't need to see. Infidelity can be felt, no proof is needed. Fakhri! Who was that Ferri who returned after fifteen years?

I didn't look up to see who had entered the bedroom, assuming it must be one of those girls coming to touch up her makeup.

"Hey, men aren't supposed to enter this room," I said.

"Not if a woman like you is here," he answered.

I felt something clawing my stomach.

Tower drank from his bottle and approached me.

"I have a husband, idiot," I said shrilly and stood stiffly up. My body was shaking.

"Shhhh." He came closer.

"I said get out, son of a bitch!" I stepped back.

He came closer, slowly, throwing the empty bottle on the bed, which had anything but water in it. He pulled at his pony tail.

"Go to hell!" My voice was trembling.

He hiccupped, wiping nose with sleeve.

I was stuck against the wall. "One more step . . . I'll scream." My chin was shaking out of control.

"Chill out, babe," he said in English, head tilted, his breath in my face sickening me. I held one hand on my mouth and another on my belly. He drew his face nearer. I didn't have enough power in my arms to push him back. I squeezed out from under his arms, which were on the wall behind and above me. He turned and grasped at my shawl. I let go of it and ran to the adjoining bathroom and locked it. Knees on the floor, I held my hands over my mouth to suffocate the sobs. Now my entire body was shaking violently. There was something bitter in my mouth and a sharp pain in my belly. I puked.

The drumming in my head came from the constant knocking on the door. I held my face under running water. "Noushin! Noushin!" Azita was calling. I noticed a bruise on my forehead when I looked in the mirror to see why it hurt so. I untied my hair to cover the bruise.

"Oh my God, what's wrong with you?" she said when I opened the door.

"Nothing, I was just feeling sick," I said, looking at the other side of the room, my hand pressing my belly.

"Pregnant?" she asked.

"What? Shut your mouth for the love of God." I winced.

"Okay. I'm sorry to say this but Amir is throwing up. He had a little too much," she said meekly.

"All right! I'll take care of that." I put a hand on her shoulder and asked her to leave me alone for a minute. Putting on my black, long manteau and headscarf I was careful not to look in the mirror. It was difficult to carry myself to the living room. Aria's arm was on his wife's shoulder and they were talking to the few guests who hadn't left yet. I didn't want to know the time. I walked towards them, trying hard to keep my balance. Mona looked back and frowned as soon as our eyes met. Aria murmured something to her that I didn't understand. Mona, with her baby face, was so pretty that night. Oh, God! How had I not seen her this whole time! How was that possible?

It was hard to keep my balance and not fall down. I couldn't find Amir, either. I thought he might be in the washroom, so I sat on one of the chairs near the door, chewing my nails.

It was all because of Mona, because I liked her so much. She was the reason I left the two alone that night. Newly pregnant, Mona couldn't stand being away from Aria, who was on a mission in the south. I asked her to come to my house. She said she felt too unwell to move. I asked my darling aunt to go with me, but she said she was too tired and preferred to go to bed. I asked Amir and he said Mona might not feel comfortable around him, and that I could comfort her alone. It was late at night when I left the house to be with Mona. I did that for Mona's sake and now she looked at me like she was looking at her father's murderer. Half an hour after arriving at her place, I was like a frying fish. I had a knowing, tormented feeling. I couldn't sit, I couldn't stand, I was going crazy but I stayed with Mona until she fell asleep. I had called a cab rather than calling Amir for a ride home. I thought I would explain that I was concerned he might be asleep.

Amir had changed his underwear and he didn't touch me at all that night. Not even for a second. Not even when I shook him and tried to wake him up. Not after I cried silently on that bed for three hours nonstop.

Finally, I found Amir. He had crashed on the kitchen table, my silk shawl under his head. I bent and put his hand around my neck to raise him. As soon as I smelled his breath, I felt sick again. I held my hand over my mouth and ran to the bathroom.

Just Like Googoosh

THE YOUNG MAN REACHED INTO his Kurdish pants pocket, pulled out some cash from among the business cards, receipts, and other folded papers, and put his small black pouch on the counter, next to the scale.

"Two thousand and three." The fruit vendor licked his upper lip on which there was a huge red moustache and looked obliquely at the man's grey, baggy pants.

The man unfolded the banknotes only to see some long, black strands of hair between them. Despite the cold, sweat dropped from his left temple onto his one-week-old beard and hollow cheeks. Then, he paused.

An old man next to him handed his shopping bags to the fruit vendor. The man with the red moustache put them on the digital scale one by one and pressed the buttons on the display. The vendor looked again at the young man who was staring at the strands of hair between his fingers.

"Two thousand and three hundred tomans!" the fruit vendor said, raising an eyebrow, startling the young man. "Two and three," the vendor repeated, looking irritated.

"Prices soar every second," the young man said, as if talking to himself.

"Been the same for the last two weeks," the vendor said.

"Here you go." The man put the strands of hair in his pocket and gave the vendor all the cash he had in his hand, and the vendor threw it into the rusted drawer of the counter under the scale.

The man picked up the bags of potatoes, onions, and eggplants. He was stepping out of the store when the cell phone in his large pocket rang. He looked at its display, which read "Chonour" and pressed the green button.

"Allo! . . . Near home . . . No! . . . Please, don't start again, please . . . You might be comfortable, but she isn't." The cold weather turned his hands crimson while he carefully picked his steps in the snow in the dark narrow alley. "Chonour! You think I have forgotten how you'd imprison yourself every time you had a few pimples on your face?" The man stopped, remembered something. He put down the grocery bags, searched his pockets one by one, turned them inside out. "Hold on," he whispered to the cell, picked up the bags and ran back to the counter where the digital scale stood.

"My pouch?" the man asked, looking around. "I had a small black pouch here."

The fruit vendor was counting some cash and did not respond. A woman in a long, Kurdish dress was bent over a box of big and almost rotten cucumbers, carefully selecting some. The man's knees hit her while he was leaving the store in a hurry, still holding the cell and the grocery bags.

"You blind?" The woman turned her head, her cheeks and nose red from the cold. The man remained speechless, looking at her thick black hair pouring out of the headscarf and onto her waist.

About ten steps further, he reached the last customer who'd left the store, an old man walking with a crutch, carrying a few tomatoes in a white bag.

"*Agha* . . . *Agha*! I had a small pouch there." The man looked at the tomatoes and pointed at the store. He didn't see when the old man shrugged because he stuck the cell to his ear and shouted, "Allo! . . . Allo!" The display was dark.

The man ran to the fruit vendor again. "*Agha*! My pouch. Didn't you see my pouch?" he implored.

The fruit vendor with a sly smile on his face took a black bag out of his rusty drawer. "Is this the one?"

The man grabbed the pouch, frowning. His cell rang again, and he answered it. "*Slaw*, sorry . . . Look! She is not in a position to party . . . she doesn't like anybody to see her."

He reached the door of a building, looked up, and stepped back. "Listen, sis, I'd like to go with you and I know that I should, but I can't leave her alone . . . Why don't you understand?"

The curtains of the fourth floor were pulled down and the lights were off. "What's that?"

He frowned, raised his head to hold the cell to his ear, took the key out of his pocket and stepped forward to open the door. "It's not *zesht*! Who the hell are these relatives anyway? Why do we have to be there for them all the time, when they left us alone after father's death? Where the hell were they when Mom was in hospital?" Closing the door, he continued talking. "Whatever! Tell them my brother can't go anywhere without his wife's permission. Tell everyone my brother is a miserable, docile, weak man. Tell 'em he's not a man at all, if that makes you happy." He pressed the red button and was about to crush the phone against the wall.

He turned on the hallway lights and noticed the loud music. He turned them on again when he reached the third floor, since they had automatically turned off. In front of the door, there were dozens of shoes. He stopped for a moment and heard the voice inside the apartment. "No one can resist dancing to this song."

The man climbed the stairs slowly, listening to the people's applause and hurrahs. He smiled. His pouch fell and slipped down three stairs. The man climbed down, picked it up and continued climbing. People inside the apartment persisted with their calls of happiness. He didn't look back any more.

When he reached the fourth floor, he buzzed and waited a few minutes. He put down the grocery bags, and tucked the black pouch under his armpit. He was turning the key in the door when a frail, slim woman in a white Kurdish dress and headscarf opened the door. Her blue velvet vest was entirely embroidered in bands of multicoloured flowers. She said hello and reached out to grab the bags.

"No, no. I'll take 'em," the man bent and kissed her forehead.

"I can," the woman whispered.

"You can," he replied. He gave her one small bag, looking at her red nose and cheeks. She went in quickly. He put the black pouch in his coat pocket, picked up the other bags and went in. She was not in the living room. He went to the kitchen. She was washing some dishes. He stayed there for a moment. "I'll wash 'em."

"I can," she said, not turning to him.

He pulled on the handle of the fridge door and said, "This is broken. I should fix it." He bent down, hands on knees, and looked inside. There was a jar and a bottle of water, a can of tuna and some bread.

"Good news!" He took the bottle and sipped the water. "Our loan is approved. See how lucky we are?" He put his hand on her shoulder. "We got absolutely nothing to worry about, *aziz*. Also, we have a chance of getting reimbursed for the new medication." She kept washing.

The man put the bottle down on the counter top, left for the bedroom and hung his coat. He took the pouch out of his pocket, stretched his hand and touched the object inside. His eyes stared into space, lips moving and right foot trembling. He looked at the kitchen door and then at the pouch. The cell rang. He saw the name "Chonour" on the display.

"Allo." He held his thumb on the red button for a few seconds. The screen went dark.

"Wrong number." He turned towards the kitchen and saw the corner of the woman's white dress quickly flitting by the door.

He crouched down, turned on the TV, picked up a video from a pile and put it into the player. The man leaned on the cushion and stretched his legs, looked at the small screen of the old TV, and glanced at the pile of moving boxes in the other corner of the room. On the top box lay a wooden framed wedding picture. The man and the woman were holding hands and smiling at the photographer. The bride's hair flowed down to her waist. No voice from the kitchen.

"Fermisk! Your beloved is singing, Fermisk!" he called out.

She came to the kitchen door, drying her hands.

"Come, sit here," he patted the carpet. She hung the towel on the handle of the door and sat where he had indicated. She looked at the TV and he at her.

"I know you don't feel too comfortable in this place but, you know, nobody knows us here and the rent is reasonable."

"I know all this." She looked at the TV screen and hummed a sad song along with Googoosh.

He tried to draw her headscarf back, but its knot kept it in place. He untied it while looking at her profile.

"I'll buy you the blue scarf I promised," he said.

"Oh, I'd forgotten about that."

"I haven't."

She held his wrist when he finished untying the scarf. He stared at her. Her face was dry but her eyes were red and her eyelids swollen. She freed his hand, and he took off her scarf and held her head across from his face. Standing on his knees, he touched her hair, took off her hairclip, and spread the hair over her shoulder. He bent her head forward and stared at the white hairless area that was spreading, taking an ever greater share of her head.

"It doesn't show, if . . . you . . . tie your hair like that." He swallowed.

"Tie what hair, Diako?" she pulled the scarf back on her head.

"Well . . . it can't go on like this."

She hummed with Googoosh. *"Bezar ghesmat konim tanhaimoono . . ."*

"You mustn't cry for this every night, *gian*," he continued. "You are not in pain any more, are you?"

"You just can't stand my hair loss, can you?" she said, still looking at Googoosh.

"What are you talking about, *aziz*?"

"I know, you have a thing for hair."

"Fermisk *gian*, you're beautiful with or without hair."

"Oh, I am not blind, Diako."

"You see . . . yes . . . I mean no . . . I mean it's not nice to have hair on some parts of your head . . . and not on the . . . ."

"Where have you hidden the mirrors? You thought I wouldn't notice," she suddenly yelled, peeling herself away from him.

"Fermisk *gian*, Fermisk." Diako held her face in his palms. "I haven't hidden anything from you."

"Yes, you have. There isn't one single mirror in this place. But I still see myself in the window. I know what I look like."

"No, you don't. You have no idea how beautiful you are," he said.

"You just said it's not nice to be bald." She put her hands on his which were still on her cheeks.

"I was just gonna say you could be like Googoosh."

"Like who?" she gaped.

"Look!" He said. "There is a show where . . . she is so attractive . . . she . . . she has shaved her hair. She's beautiful, isn't she?"

"She hasn't quite shaved her head. But, that's a very short haircut which I have always liked. You never let me cut my hair short like that."

"You'll love it!" He hesitated. "It would be . . . great . . . Let's try it . . . you will look super attractive. I am sure."

She wiped a tear in the corner of her eye. "You remember my childhood picture with shaved hair?" She smiled.

"I do. You looked even prettier than Googoosh." He kissed her hand.

She ran her hand through her hair and looked down at the mass of black strands in her fingers. "Heh, I did that to my hair after I watched that clip of Googoosh you just talked about. My mom beat me up." She smirked. "I will look like a boy, you're not gonna like . . ."

He kissed her on her lips.

She drew her head back. "Hey, I was in my childhood streets last night."

"Where?"

"Those old streets. I dreamt there was a flood." She leaned her head on his shoulder. "The water was very clean but they said it was sewage. I was in it."

"Who said so?" He patted her head.

"I don't know."

"Was I in your dream, too?"

"I was all by myself," she said, shaking her head.

They were both silent.

"Diako?" she asked.

"*Gian?*" He gently patted her head.

"If I ever get better . . ."

"You will, *bawanm*, you will, and your beautiful hair will grow back," he kissed her forehead.

"Say, what did you say to my mom?"

"I told her the truth."

"You told her the truth?" She lifted her head and looked into his eyes.

"Not like that! She said she's gonna visit. I tried to tell her something so she would not be surprised when she sees you with a headscarf at home," he said.

"Oh, what did you say, then?" Fermisk asked.

"I said you have been to a contaminated swimming pool."

"She knows I don't swim."

"Well, I said you had been there once," he said.

"You think she believed you?"

"What else could I say?"

"Don't know," she shrugged. "I'll never tell her the truth."

"We shouldn't. She can't take it."

"I'll put on one of those scarves with a hat for my brother's memorial day."

"Do so, *azizam*."

"Buy me a wig."

"I will, *gianakam*." He pulled her in his arms.

"What colour will you buy?"

"The colour of your own hair," he said.

"Naah, buy me a new colour, but a nice one." She put her hand through her hair then looked down at the clump she had brought out. "Let's stick this hair in again and not pay extra money for the wig," she laughed. He squeezed her and pressed his cheek to her pale cheek.

"Hey, don't break my bones."

"Let me bring a sheet."

"All right," she said.

He fetched his small black pouch and a sheet and sat behind Fermisk.

Diako spread the white sheet on the floor. She sat in the middle of it, facing the TV screen. He withdrew a silver metal object out of the black bag and took its two long handles between his thumb and forefinger. He stood on his knees, held Fermisk's hair between his hands, swallowed, lifted her hair and covered his face in it. Fermisk turned to him. Diako saw his reflection in the screen of the television.

"Turn," he said.

"Why don't *you* turn?" Fermisk asked.

"Turn, please."

She placed her palms on the carpet and turned her body around. Diako sat on his knees. He took her hair in his left hand and the metal piece in his right. He stood up, sat down again, and stood up once more. Diako fetched a chair, placed it behind her and sat down on it. "Sit on your knees."

"Yes, *Ghorban!*"

He put her hair on his lap. Then, he gently pulled the strands above her ear towards himself and put them on the bald part of her head. Diako placed his fingers on Fermisk's forehead and pushed her head back on his lap. She resisted. He kissed the place between her brows. Her eyes were shut, her cheeks wet. He pushed her head forward tenderly and started from where the bald spot was spreading in her hair. The silver-white cold metal went on and on. The hair was falling on his knee and on the white sheet. His hands were trembling. "Just like Googoosh," he whispered.